THE GREAT CATSBY

A NOLA TAIL MYSTERY BOOK #1

B.K. BAXTER

BRIXBAXTER PUBLISHING

The Great Catsby

A Nola Tail Mystery Book #1

First Edition.

Cover Designer: Jeff Brown
Editor: Eric Martinez

FIND B.K. BAXTER

www.bkbaxterbooks.com

PROLOGUE

The old plantation house was big, meaning it at least had size working in its favor. It was much larger than our old one-bedroom apartment in Baltimore, but bigger wasn't always better. Just ask Jade, who seemed less than enamored with my own superior size. She was always moaning that she needed to start lifting weights to be able to pick me up.

Jade and I were getting settled into our new home in the exotic-sounding province of New Orleans, Louisiana. The air was heavier here, laden with moisture that made my fur frizz. I was used to Baltimore's climate. While humid in the summer, we'd also had a snowy winter. The climate in Louisiana made me feel like I was walking through Jello.

Jello was another food Jade wouldn't let me eat.

For a roommate, she was decent enough. She kept me fed, even if she ignored my schedule, despite my insistent regular reminders. And she always remembered my favorite kibble. It was the delicacies reserved for the creatures that walked on two legs that she and I didn't see eye to eye on.

Why she refused to share the ham on her sandwich or to let me get a taste of the cream she was pouring into her coffee, I would never know. It was probably related to my impressive size and her envy of me.

And while we're on the topic of all things edible, the food here in Louisiana was different too. Scents of various spices unknown to my nostrils before we'd strayed this far down south were appearing to greet me every day. It kept my nose busy, and my brain, as I determined which new tasty tidbits to try and how to beg, swallow, or steal them.

Despite my excitement at a novel culinary journey, it was still difficult to settle into a new routine. I found myself gazing out the dusty windows past trees that looked too lazy to hold up their own leaves. I was homesick for the busy streets of Baltimore.

Out here, the only thing I saw out my windows were nutria slowly hauling their fat rat bodies across the lawn in the daytime heat like Mr. Hanes, the old man in 4B back in our old building, hauling himself across the summer sidewalk.

Back in Baltimore, my favorite pastime was sitting in the front window that looked out over the sidewalk and hissing at the dogs when they passed. The smart ones always whined and hunched back on themselves. The stupid ones barked, running in circles and getting their owners entangled in their leashes. I'd once seen a Pekingese catch her leash on her owner's heel, causing said owner to tumble into a puddle and let out a string of curses filthier than the maintenance man when he couldn't get the sink to unclog.

That little episode had kept me in stitches for a week. But really, it wasn't fair of me to laugh. Dogs were idiots. No wonder they needed their owners to lead them around everywhere, lest they get lost or go haring off after anything with a pulse that crossed their path. We cats were much more refined. We didn't have owners. We had roommates. And we didn't need anyone to guide us around at the end of a string.

Strings were prey.

Maybe the size of this place wasn't the benefit I thought it was. It meant more territory to protect. Back in Baltimore, I only had to worry about the small enclosed backyard that belonged to the apartment complex and my bent-eared nemesis, an old gray tabby male that insisted on encroaching on my domain.

My yowls against him were legendary, as was the bout of fisticuffs we'd come to the time I'd managed to escape the apartment and caught him on the fence. Unfortunately, Jade insisted that I act like a gentleman, so we'd yet to have a rematch. But I batted at the window like a champion whenever I saw him, and I'd like to think he feared me from afar.

Still, I preferred to see this rambling old structure as an upgrade. One that afforded me certain advantages. Like the unexpected exit to the outdoors that Jade had yet to find. I used to have to wait for my chance to dash out the door when Jade wasn't expecting it, but she'd gotten pretty good at blocking me over the years we've cohabitated. But the broken window at the far end of the basement allowed me secret access to the fairyland that was now mine to claim.

I'd already done a reconnaissance mission to get my bearings and had unearthed a town buried in the past. In Baltimore, I'd had to be mindful not to run afoul of the traffic or Sir Chonksworth the Bold would become Sir Chonk the Flat. Although I often tried to run off with one of Jade's pancakes, I didn't want to become one. But the traffic in New Orleans was like a mouse that hated cheese: it didn't exist.

The main street had only one stoplight in the center of the town, the bones of which were laid 275 cat generations ago, or around six human generations. Not every structure was that ancient, but none were exactly what I would call modern. Especially the old library where Jade had started her job as assistant librarian.

Why she chose to surround herself with books instead of more interesting things like moths, catnip, or even boxes, I'll never understand. She always had her nose buried in her books. Back in Baltimore, she'd read aloud from one to me every night. Mostly, I slept on her lap, but the stories still managed to sink in.

And what ridiculous stories they were. The authors never spent enough time on the most interesting parts. No discussion of hunting for small furry things or chittering at birds. No mention of the ecstasy of burying your nails in corrugated cardboard. Just silly things like love and betrayal and regret.

And sometimes murder.

At least those stories were a little intriguing. Cats were well-built instinct machines, and the desire to feel a heartbeat slow under our teeth was one we all shared. Despite our killer instincts, we still craved affection from those closest to us. But that didn't mean we liked to hear about all that mushy human emotional nonsense.

The New Orleans Public Library was housed in a historic building that was slowly crumbling in the moist Louisiana heat. Still, the space itself was pristine, likely thanks to the elderly woman charged with bossing my roommate around. Jade might grumble about her after work as she debated with herself over whether to have a second glass of wine with dinner, but no one could argue that the head librarian ran a tight ship.

Across the street from the library was City Hall, a square building built of stone in the center of a manicured lawn that stretched for an entire block. The corners of the square were decorated with archaic cannons that, like my roommate, hadn't seen any action in years.

I'd already spent several nights wandering the town. I'd passed a drug store with its bright green cross. A grocery store that smelled fresher than our local bodega, with signs advertising sales on things I'd never heard of like white hominy and gumbo base. A restaurant that reeked of eons of grease that seemed to have soaked into every pore.

Not that I was complaining. I'd spent an hour exploring the dumpster behind that place and managed to find a couple choice treasures. But the days of grooming required afterward proved those treasures weren't worth the trouble.

There were other buildings that weren't unlike the ones I'd seen in Baltimore the few times I'd managed to make it onto the streets. A church. A school. A building to repair those noisy automobiles humans seemed to love, and a building to feed them. Offices. Houses. Businesses.

It might be smaller than Baltimore, but it had all the requisite pieces to make it livable for Jade. People in New Orleans seemed friendly enough as well. They were polite, always showing their entire mouth full of teeth but not in an aggressive way. They might talk funny, but all humans and their insistence on words sounded foolish.

So why did I feel like Jade was getting herself into something she might not be able to handle here in the Deep South?

The secrets. I could smell them. Some were buried far beneath the soil of this sleepy town, but some weren't so deep. Some were very near the surface, just waiting to be discovered. Jade might not be able to tell, but I could.

Things weren't as they seemed in New Orleans.

It was a good thing I was here to keep Jade safe. And to ferret out the secrets one by one. Sir Chonksworth the Bold loved nothing more than a good mystery. And I knew that it wouldn't be long until some secret scratched its way into the light.

In the meantime, I'd keep Jade company in this big old house, patrolling its halls and its grounds, making sure she kept us fed, and angling for the occasional scratch behind the ears. Some things might be vastly different about this place, but some things away stayed the same. Like the fact that a good scratch behind my ears always made me purr.

Not all secrets were bad. Some ended in new discoveries that bring us closer together.

Me? I planned on discovering the secret of how to snag one of those oyster po'boys I'd heard about. As long as Jade didn't discover my emergency exit.

My roommate was clever, but she tended to get distracted. It was up to me to make sure she focused on the important things. Speaking of, it was about time to let her know the food bowl was empty again.

It was a quandary, how that kibble always seemed to disappear so fast. I might be able to uncover long-buried secrets, but the secret of never-ending kibble was a mystery I had yet to solve.

CHAPTER 1

"Sure, her family may have been here for over a century, but that doesn't mean they've ever had an ounce of class."

I was working my way through a stack of returned books, half-heartedly listening to Dottie's stories as I wondered at how even the air conditioning couldn't keep the Louisiana heat at bay. I would never understand why Uncle Mike had chosen this out of the way hamlet that could have stood right inside the gates of Hell based on its temperature alone.

Miss Dottie Turleigh often stopped by the library as she made her rounds, and today, she'd decided to keep me company as I went about my duties. I didn't mind since Dottie seemed like a rather harmless old lady to me, a relic on par with our surroundings.

I'd met her the first day I'd started my part-time assistant librarian job at the New Orleans Public Library. She'd been wearing a long-sleeved dress made of heavy fabric that would have given me heat stroke if I'd worn it for even five minutes, and a jaunty little hat had been perched on her nest of gray curls. She'd even been wearing delicate lace gloves, completing the look of a woman who could have walked out of the pages of a decades old *Ladies Home Journal* issue.

She'd introduced herself to me and smiled, revealing twin rows of perfectly pearly-white dentures. I'd quickly learned during that first meeting that she might know as much about my Uncle Mike as I did. My uncle wasn't the limit of her knowledge however. Dottie Turleigh seemed to know the biography of nearly everyone in Saint Dismas Parish.

Her true talent lay in her delivery, the hushed matter-of-fact tone she considered appropriate for spilling others' secrets coupled with the butter-wouldn't-melt-in-my-mouth-despite-the-heat look on her sweet-old-woman face.

Dottie was currently regaling me with the details of her ongoing feud with a neighbor whose dog preferred Dottie's yard for doing its business. This wasn't the first time she'd had words with her neighbor. Apparently, they'd clashed since grade school when they'd both taken first communion at the same time and the neighbor girl had stepped on Dottie's veil, ripping it and causing Dottie's mother to, "pitch a fit loud enough that Daddy had to lock her up in the bedroom and put her to bed with one of his little blue pills."

I wasn't quite sure what to make of Dottie and the picture she painted of New Orleans. When I'd arrived in town almost a month ago, I'd recently suffered the biggest shock of my life after learning I'd inherited an antebellum plantation house from my newly deceased uncle. An uncle I'd barely known, I should add. His death had brought me to this small town on the banks of the Mississippi River, a town where time seemed to move as slowly as the swirls and eddies of the muddy currents that flowed by it.

Baltimore was by no means the center of the universe, but the pace of big-city life had not prepared me for a town that looked to be only a few blocks long when I first arrived. I quickly realized that its confines sprawled beyond the compact downtown area, stretching to include massive, majestic houses like the one I'd inherited. Stately and steeped in history, these mansions had once been occupied by women swallowed by the yards of fabric that made up their hoop skirts and men who dueled with pistols to defend their family's honor. Or so I imagined.

Ages had passed since those halcyon days before the War of

Northern Aggression, as I'd heard it called since I'd arrived in Louisiana, but I could still see the ghosts of that bygone era all around me. This library, for example, had once been the railroad depot before the lines had merged and converted to freight only. They'd no longer needed a waiting room for passengers, so the city had converted the old brick building into a library. Its ancient wooden benches had been exchanged for shelves, although a few still lined the walls under the front windows where the occasional patron would sit and read.

The rectangular brick building sat along Main Street, its front facing City Hall, its back still lined with ghost tracks that were no longer in use. Its windows were trimmed in white, and its entry doors were a glossy emerald green with matching lamps suspended from the overhang above them. The first time I'd seen the New Orleans Public Library, I thought it didn't look like much, especially after the Enoch Pratt Free Library, the block-long stone edifice that was one of the most beautiful buildings in the city of Baltimore. It had several stories lined with endless shelves, and although I'd only been a junior cataloger there, I'd felt like I was part of some vast machinery that brought hallowed knowledge to the masses.

I didn't think the little one-story building in New Orleans could hold even a quarter of the periodicals section of my old library, and the "machinery" of my new library consisted of myself, the head librarian, and a cleaning woman who came twice a week to empty the trash and mop out the bathrooms. And as for bringing knowledge to the masses, I'd quickly learned that the majority of our patrons devoured a diet comprised exclusively of paperback romance novels and lurid true-crime tales.

Still, I had to admit that the library, like the town, was growing on me. The only part of the job I didn't enjoy was sitting in her office, clicking slowly through the screens on her ancient computer. Head Librarian Luanne Jackson greeted my natural enthusiasm with arms crossed and brow furrowed. Luanne didn't seem to have a sense of humor. Or an ounce of patience. Or even basic human kindness. She felt affection for her collection. Anyone or anything else was viewed with suspicion and annoyance.

I heard her chunky heels start to pound against the wooden floor outside her office and held back a sigh. Luanne approached the circulation desk, blasting poor old Dottie with a glare that made the busybody's grin evaporate. Without even saying goodbye, Dottie fled the library, on to greener pastures like the beauty salon or the fabric store where she could gossip without interruption.

"We're out of two-sided tape."

I blinked at Luanne's announcement. "I'm sorry. Shall I..." I'd never been tasked with providing supplies before. Luanne was in charge of ordering, and so far, I wasn't allowed near the single credit card the library was allowed for its purchases.

"I need the tape if I'm going to finish labeling the new acquisitions."

I nodded when I realized she wasn't going to say anything else. Luanne was a woman of few words, most of them resembling snarls. When the silence stretched between us, I finally recognized that she was waiting for me to speak. But I knew nothing of our two-sided tape suppliers. "How can I help?"

"You can go find some darn tape." She slapped down the credit card. "Bring back the receipt, and no funny business with the card."

Her heels punished the floor as she walked away. I picked up the card, amazed at this new level of trust between us. A few steps out the green doors and I was on Main Street, feeling like I was drowning in the late afternoon humidity. It was only spring, but it felt like the depths of late summer in Baltimore or worse. I hurried down the block, wanting to return to air conditioning as quickly as possible.

I'd only been in New Orleans for a few weeks, so I still wasn't entirely familiar with the offerings of the retail establishments located near the library. One place I'd been a handful of times already was the Tip Top Grocery, only a few blocks away. I opened the door and walked inside, letting out a breath of relief as the cold air hit me.

It only took about ten minutes to investigate all the shelves, and there was no sign of two-sided tape. There was a limited selection of transparent tape and duct tape, but I knew if I returned from my mission with anything other than what Luanne had ordered, I wouldn't be doing myself any favors.

I made my way to the small checkout stand, one of only two in the store, and waved to the owner. I'd met Sally on my first day in New Orleans when I'd come seeking sustenance. The drive down to Louisiana had put me off food that came in a bag or a Styrofoam container, so I'd come to the Tip Top Grocery to grab something green and fresh.

Sally Tennyson was in her late forties, with carrot-red hair that showed just the tiniest hint of white at the temples. Round glasses with an almost invisible frame sat on her button nose, which was also decorated by a smattering of freckles that spread from her nose to her rosy cheeks. A friendly woman, Sally had told me she got her meat and produce fresh from local producers, a point of pride. I figured if she had any two-sided tape lying around, she'd be willing to spare some for New Orleans's newest arrival.

"Hey there, Jade," she said, her southern drawl serving to make her sound even more friendly. "Something I can help you find today?"

"Yes, there is. I'm hoping you have some two-sided tape."

Her smile remained as she shook her head. "I sure am sorry, but I don't carry that sort of tape. I do have a couple other kinds though. Maybe they will work?" She started to come out from her station but I held up my hand, stopping her.

"It's not for me. It's for the library, and I think Luanne has her heart set on the two-sided kind."

"Oh." Sally nodded in agreement. "If that woman has a heart, I'm sure you're right."

I let out a laugh. "Unfortunately, the technology at the library only detects barcodes, not anatomy, so we'll never know for certain."

Sally chuckled at my lame librarian joke, and I liked her even more than I already had. "You might try the drug store. Mercer's got a collection of odds and ends in there."

I thanked her for the suggestion. At a noise from the back of the store, my head turned, and I saw a young man in a blue apron carrying a crate of fruit toward the produce section. He had close-cropped light brown hair with matching brown eyes and appeared to be a couple years younger than me.

I watched as he set the crates down, then carefully scooped up a spider that was tucked in among the apples in the top crate. He carried the long-legged creature outside and set it gently on the ground. I was struck by the gesture.

If I found a bug at home, I set Chonks on it. Sometimes, the lazy cat would stop sleeping enough to take the creepy crawly out. Either that or I would avoid the room where the insect was discovered for as long as I could.

Sally noticed the young man as he came back through the door and called him over. "Stanley, I'd like you to meet Jade Hastings, the new librarian."

His eyes lit up at the word *librarian* and he stuck his big hand out in front of him. I shook it, then added that I was the assistant librarian, lest he get delusions of my grandeur.

"Stanley loves reading. Don't you?" I noticed that Sally altered her tone, almost as if she were speaking to a child.

"Is that right?" I asked, mostly just to say something.

Stanley nodded but remained silent, an earnest grin on his face. I wondered if maybe he was differently abled, despite his clear-eyed understanding of our conversation.

"Well, if that's the case, you should stop by the library tonight at five. We're holding the first meeting of New Orleans's brand-new book club. Would you like to join us?"

He nodded again, although this time with more restraint.

"Go ahead and finish with the fruits," Sally said.

He did as she asked.

Then Sally hooked her elbow through mine and started walking us toward the door. He's very shy, you know?" she told me in a hushed tone as she led me out of the store. "But I'll be there, and I'll do my best to drag him along."

"Great," I said, unsure if it actually would be. New Orleans's response to its newest book club so far seemed to be indifference. But at least no one was hostile, except maybe the head librarian. "I look forward to seeing you later!"

The drug store wasn't far, and I covered the distance in as near of a sprint as I could, trying to avoid gathering a pool of sweat in the small of my back. For some reason, that always made me feel slightly disgusted. My hygiene wasn't what I would call pristine, but I did have my limits.

A large green cross decorated the window next to a pair of eyes bigger than my head, advertising a brand of reading glasses. The eyes were so faded, I knew the glasses wouldn't be able to help them see again. *Mercer Drug* flashed in neon cursive down the side of the building, another nod to an era long past.

Inside, I wandered the aisles, taking some time to acquaint myself with the layout of items. As a librarian, I craved orderly shelves, but it appeared drug stores weren't held to the same standard as libraries. Shampoos were stocked next to bug repellent. Antacids sat next to clearance flip-flops. My brain couldn't process the logic of the store, and my hopes of finding the mythical tape of the two-sided variety were sinking.

"Looking for something?"

A handsome man in his late fifties or early sixties came around the corner, his smile warm. He was wearing a white coat embroidered with the name *Patrick,* and I assumed he was the pharmacist.

"Two-sided tape. I'm the new assistant librarian, and we need it for our new acquisitions."

"Ah yes," he said, nodding. "I heard there was someone new in town. You're Mike Hasting's niece."

"I am," I said, quickly refocusing the conversation. It could be a little startling, having everyone already know your backstory. "About the tape? I'm afraid Luanne will be pretty disappointed if I don't come back with some, and I already tried the Tip Top."

"I've got some. Hang on." He disappeared, giving me time for another attempt at cataloging the assembled items for purchase. But I just couldn't see how putting the hairbrushes next to the batteries made any sense.

"I've been waiting for Luanne to call me for a delivery but it looks like she has a new lackey," he said with a smile, holding out two rolls of the tape I'd been hunting for.

"Looks like you're right," I said, taking the tape and starting my journey toward the cash register. "I don't mind the occasional errand as long as it's air-conditioned."

Patrick laughed at my joke, and I started to wonder if I had a career in stand-up comedy. Maybe it was just that the people of New Orleans were starved for something to laugh at.

Oh goodie, that's me.

CHAPTER 2

The crowd was larger than I expected for the inaugural meeting of the New Orleans Book Club. They trickled in as I was closing the library. I'd set the club meeting for a day I knew Luanne would be going home early.

To say the head librarian was resistant to change would be like saying the Mississippi River was a trickle of sweat between my shoulder blades. To give the club a chance, I thought it best to make sure Luanne wasn't around when we kicked things off.

We sat in a circle, the chairs stolen from nearby tables and arranged on the large rug that set off the children's area. I scanned the group, realizing that I recognized only a few faces. Taking a deep breath, I pushed past my nerves and began.

"Welcome, everyone, to the first meeting of the New Orleans Book Club. We'll be reading classics of literature and discussing them each week in an open and inclusive environment. Before we get started, we should go around the room and introduce ourselves. I'll start."

My gaze made its way around the circle, stopping to make eye contact with each person before moving on. "My name is Jade Hastings, and I recently moved to New Orleans from Baltimore. I might be new in town, but some of you might have known my uncle, Michael Hastings."

There were a couple nods when I mentioned my uncle but mostly blank looks. I wondered what Uncle Mike was doing down here if it wasn't making friends.

"I've always loved to read," I continued, "and I'm excited to meet like-minded neighbors."

I nodded to the woman on my left, who grinned and introduced herself. "I think most everyone here knows me already, but my name is Dr. Charlotte Rains. Most people call me Char." She looked around the circle a little defiantly. "I'm an avid reader, and I'm looking forward to re-reading some good books."

Char was a few years older than me, definitely young for a doctor, but friendlier than most of her kind that I'd interacted with. Her hair was a dark auburn, cut in a bob around her face, and her light brown eyes were kind.

After the doctor came Dottie, someone everyone in the room was definitely already acquainted with. Dottie greeted the rest of the folks assembled, then took over half the introduction of the woman sitting next to her.

"Everyone knows Alma," she said, putting her gloved hand on the woman's arm. "She's the mayor's wife, of course."

Alma nodded, her eyes bright and her fingers tapping against her knees. Her blonde hair was streaked with gray and slowly tumbling out of the loose bun resting on her neck. "Yes, Mayor Travis is my husband, has been for the past twenty-five years. I helped run his campaign, you might remember. We've always been big supporters of the library, and…"

I nodded, waiting for the woman to run out of steam. I was just about to step in, as rude as it seemed, when the young woman sitting on her right interrupted for me.

"We know, Miss Alma, and everyone thinks your husband is doin' a bang-up job, but if we wanna do any talkin' about the book tonight, maybe we should get past the saying hello phase?"

Alma touched her forehead and tittered nervously while Tabby, as the young woman called herself, launched into her own introduction. "Y'all already know me, so I'll keep it brief. Name's Tabby, and I didn't do much reading in school because I had better things to do, but Vince figures it's time for me to get a little so-called refinement, so I'm here."

She was beautiful in a cubic-zirconium-in-the-rough sort of way, with platinum-blonde hair that fell in waves that hit her tanned shoulders. Tabby was statuesque, well built, and had a natural confidence that was evidenced in every move of her toned body.

Tabby shrugged at the silence that greeted her, then looked to the woman to her right, who just happened to be one of the familiar faces.

"I'm Sally," she said with a little wave. "Me and Stanley are over from the Tip Top."

Stanley, the only male face in the crowd, nodded along. He was dressed in the same outfit as earlier, minus the apron, and I noticed the T-shirt he was wearing featured the cartoon Tasmanian devil and his trademark sloppy grin.

Tabby let out a chuckle. "You got Taz to come to the library?"

Sally's grin shrank. "Stanley likes the library. He spends a fair amount of time here, unlike you."

Tabby held up her hands in surrender. "That's the truth."

A well-put-together older brunette interrupted, and I was relieved for the help. I was beginning to realize that keeping this group focused might be a challenge.

"My name is Dinah Mercer. I'm President of the Society for Historical Preservation here in New Orleans and a real estate agent. This book club is a wonderful way to bring the community together in such a noble pursuit."

Tabby yawned. It was loud and visual and earned half an eye roll from Dinah.

We'd finally made our way around the circle, and the final introduction belonged to an attractive dark-haired woman with copper skin who seemed to have no problem following Tabby's disruption. "I'm Mercy Means. You've probably noticed my jewelry on display at the New Orleans Bazaar."

Mercy held up an arm to display an intricate bracelet, then put her palms underneath her dangly earrings. Heads turned when Tabby started making a gagging sound.

Mercy's chin lifted as her eyes narrowed, and she let out a sniff.

"That's enough," Dinah hissed at Tabby. "This isn't how you behave in polite company."

Tabby gave her a look, crossing her arms over already-crossed legs and letting her flip-flop dangle off her foot. It was clear she was disinterested in the opinions of those gathered around her.

"Okay," I said at last, "it's nice to meet all of you." Bending down to grab the book I'd placed under my chair, I held it up for the club members. "So how far did you get in our first selection, *The Great Gatsby*?"

I'd advertised the first book on the flyers and online announcements of the club, but I hadn't expected many to actual crack it open prior to the initial meeting. It seemed I had predicted correctly because my question remained suspended in the quiet air.

Finally, Char raised her hand. "I only made it through the first chapter, but I read it back in high school, so I remember the main points."

A couple mumbles from around the circle let her know that Char wasn't the only one who'd made it through the high school's required reading list.

"Don't you just love the cover?" Dottie crooned. "She reminds me of myself, coming out as a debutante years ago. I'd insisted on red lipstick, even though Mama said ladies didn't wear that shade. It caused a minor scandal." She let out a high twitter of laughter.

I held on to my smile, just barely, and nodded at the older woman. "Yes, the cover has been talked about for decades, its symbolism discussed at length. Its image, taken from Dr. T.J. Eckleburg's billboard in the book, ties into some of the major themes of the book. Does anyone want to mention any of the book's themes?"

I was beginning to think that no one would speak, but then Stanley raised his hand, and it trembled gently as it hung in the air. I nodded to encourage him, and after a moment, he began to speak, haltingly at first.

"The main theme is the American Dream or its fallacy. Gatsby's journey from a nobody to the man everyone wants to be is all built on lies. Everyone in the book traffics in lies, either lies they tell others or lies they tell themselves. It's a book that juxtaposes the haves and have-nots, the glitter and the ash, those who empathize with others and those who have sympathy for only themselves. It is both the belief in hope and in the necessity for that hope to end."

Amazed silence greeted his words, and I got the impression that no one here had heard him speak this way, including Sally.

"You should talk more often, Taz," Tabby said, leaning over to put a hand on his leg. Stanley blushed, shying away from her touch.

I was surprised by the tone of Mercy's voice and the vitriol I heard lurking in it. "Leave that boy alone," the dark-haired woman said. "Don't you already have enough guys dangling on your string?"

Tabby shot the dark-haired woman an evil look. "You're just jealous that your husband likes me better than he ever liked you."

A few gasps hit the air and my fingers tightened on the book I was holding.

"Ex-husband," Mercy snarled, standing up suddenly. "Why are you even here, Tabby? We all know you can't read."

Tabby laughed. "I can read better than you can screw, which I hear needs improvement. I told you I'm here to get a little culture. And honestly, I thought something as boring as this would at least have wine to get butts in the seats."

"Okay, I think this is a good place to pause," I said, rising from my seat and pasting on a smile for the benefit of the folks in the circle. "We can reconvene next week. Please try and finish the first three chapters by then."

I'd expected folks to make a quick exit, considering the tension in the room, but I'd misjudged the audience. The women milled around, talking in small groups and shooting glances at Mercy and Tabby, who were now giving each other a wide berth. Sally tapped my shoulder and I turned, relieved that at least one person in attendance still wanted to talk to me after the preceding debacle.

"Thank you for starting this group, Miss Jade," she said, her hands coming around me suddenly until I was enfolded in a hug. "I haven't heard Stanley speak this much in ages."

I scanned the room to spot the subject of our conversation, and I found Stanley browsing the New Releases shelf.

"Why doesn't he talk much?" I asked, hoping the question wasn't rude.

The corners of Sally's lips turned down. "He had a rough childhood. I think that had something to do with it. But I'm not a psychiatrist, so don't quote me on it."

Taz bent down to pull a book off the shelf, and when he straightened, he started, noticing that Tabby had approached him while he was distracted.

"How's about I give you a lift home?" Tabby asked, running a finger down the front of Stanley's T-shirt. "I'm going in that direction, and you'll have to walk otherwise."

Sally frowned, and when she spoke, it was like she was talking to herself, her voice low and her words mumbled. "I'm sure it's fine. He takes groceries out there all the time. That girl might be trouble, but Stanley is harmless."

She blinked, then turned back to me. "Well, anyway, I better get home before the mosquitos wake up since I'm walking. Thanks again." Another wave and she headed toward the exit, following behind Tabby and Stanley as they sailed out the green doors.

"Whatever happened to your uncle?"

I turned and realized the question was coming from the older woman in the designer pantsuit. Dinah looked like she spent hours making sure every hair was in place and unmovable as a mountain.

"He passed. Cancer."

"I'm sorry to hear that," she said, her face not showing any evidence of regret. "Does that mean you're now in possession of his property?"

I nodded. "He left it to me, which is why I moved down to Louisiana."

"It's a fine example of antebellum architecture," Dinah stated. "I would love a tour."

She was intense. It was a lot for me right then. "I'm sorry, but I need to put the room back in order. Thanks for coming."

I turned and started carrying chairs back to the tables to which they belonged. Char lent a hand, helping to put the room back to rights. By the time we'd finished, we were the only two people left in the library.

"Sorry about that introduction by fire," the doctor said with a chuckle. "Our town might be little, but it isn't exactly quaint."

It was my turn to laugh. "With a group this spirited, we're bound to have some good discussions," I said, hoping to convey some optimism.

"Sure. They just might not be about the book." Char put her bag over her shoulder. "You free tomorrow? We could grab some lunch and I could fill you in on exactly what you're getting into with this lively cast of characters?"

"I'd like that," I said, meaning it. I might have a couple acquaintances in New Orleans, but so far, none had crossed the line into friendship. And as the doctor seemed to be about the most normal person I'd run into yet, she could prove a good start.

"Great. Meet me at Sparky's at noon." Char departed, and I stopped by the circulation desk to gather my things.

As I locked the library doors, I realized I'd just had more interaction with patrons than I had during my entire employment at the Enoch Pratt Free Library back in Baltimore. I'd always wanted to move from cataloger to librarian, to share my love of books with the public. I'd just never envisioned a public that might take more joy out of the drama arising from the discussion of the books instead of the drama in the books themselves.

I knew one thing for certain. The New Orleans Book Club wasn't going to be boring.

CHAPTER 3

Sparky's Diner was the kind of place I would happily drive past to find a chain restaurant where I knew the bathrooms would be clean and the menu adequate. The sign out front was dingy, as were the sun-worn booths. Walking through the door, I was hit with the smell of grease that seemed to be baked into every surface.

I slid into a booth, then wiped my fingers on a paper napkin from the metal dispenser after touching the menu. It was sticky, the laminated page covered in a spilled sugary drink. Leaning over the table to peer down at the menu, I frowned at the misspellings and limited offerings.

Lunch consisted of several "baskets." Hamburger basket. Cheeseburger basket. BLT basket. Turkey and swiss basket. Fried fish basket. Fried chicken basket. And something called a "muffaletta basket," whatever that was. I saw no mention of a salad.

Guess my diet starts tomorrow. Just like yesterday.

An attractive waitress appeared beside the booth, her jaws working. She was chewing gum, which went along well with her disinterested demeanor. "What can I get you, hon?" she asked, her pencil tapping against her order pad.

The nametag on her faded pink uniform said "Presley" and I

wondered if it was a nod to the late great singer who'd been affectionately known as "Elvis the Pelvis" by some fans.

"Could you bring me a glass of ice water? I'm waiting for someone to join me."

She turned without a word, and I wondered if I was experiencing some of that famed southern hospitality I'd heard so much about. Presley reappeared and set down the water. Then she stalked off toward the kitchen. I saw that she wore kitten heels and I wondered how she stayed on her feet all day in them. I only wore heels when forced. Then again, I didn't have the waitress's legs.

Uncle Mike might have called them "great gams." I had only met my uncle a handful of times, but I'd always been amused at his antiquated vocabulary as well as his wandering eye. He'd once told the girl behind the counter of the ice-cream shop he took me to for my tenth birthday that he'd never seen a broad with sweeter stems.

I looked out the window to New Orleans's quiet downtown but there wasn't much to see. A few storefronts, an elderly woman sitting on a bus bench, knitting needles in hand. In the distance, I caught the occasional bright glint off the Mississippi's muddy waters. It was quite a change from Baltimore, but I hadn't yet made up my mind if it was a good change or a bad one. Maybe it was just mediocre.

"Gonna let me off early tonight, Sparky?"

I turned my head to stare through the cutout that opened into the kitchen, where a man in a hairnet with patchy gray stubble prepared baskets of artery-clogging lunch for his patrons.

He grunted, causing Presley to pout, hands on her faded pink hips. "You know I got that thing tonight. I gotta look nice."

"Speed dating in Baton Rouge ain't a thing, Lee," Sparky said as he set a plate in the window. "I ain't got no one to cover the end of the dinner rush if I let you go early."

"It's Wednesday," Presley countered. "Ain't gonna be no dinner rush. Now you know I never ask you for anything—"

"You asked for last Thursday afternoon off. And the week before, you had to take your mama to Shreveport on Friday, and I had to ask Della to come lend a hand. You know she hates that."

"That's because you need a pry bar to get your wife's ass off the couch," Presley said.

"No gripin' about Della, Lee. She covered for you and didn't say an unkind word."

"Della's a saint then," Presley said, throwing her hands up and stomping out of the kitchen. She was back at my table in less than a minute. "Made up your mind yet?"

I blinked, then tried on a smile. "I'm sorry. I'm still waiting for my—"

She was walking away before I finished my sentence. I heard her back in the kitchen shortly after.

"Come on, Sparky. I'll come in on Sunday morning to make up for it."

Sparky let out a burst of air through his pressed-together lips. "Don't give me that old promise. You ain't once shown up for a Sunday-morning shift."

"Can you blame me for likin' to go dancin' on Saturday nights?" Presley tried a different tack, her aggression replaced with a little-girl voice. "I'll wash your truck and clean the garbage out of the bed. How long's it been since someone did that for you?"

Sparky sighed but finally gave in to her wheedling. "Fine, you can leave early if you roll all the silverware and fill up all them sugar containers."

"Done!" she said, then leaned over to kiss his flushed cheek. "Thanks, Spark!"

The waitress had a smile on her face when she returned to my booth. "What's it gonna be, hon?"

I was just about to tell her for the third time that I was waiting for someone when the diner door opened and Char rushed in.

"Sorry!" she said, a bit breathless as she slid into the booth. Char looked at Presley and gave her a grin. "Let me get a muffaletta basket and some sweet tea." The doctor looked over at me. "What'd you order?"

"I was... uh... waiting for you to show. I'm not sure yet."

"Bring her a muffaletta basket too."

Presley nodded and made her way to the kitchen, her heels clicking on the linoleum. I focused my gaze on Char, who was typing on her phone.

"I'm so sorry," she said after a moment, tucking her phone in her pocket. "Today has been an absolute bear."

"Busy with patients?"

Char shook her head, then took a gulp of the sweet tea Presley put in front of her. "I wish. But most folks in town don't trust the 'girl doc.' They still go to old Dr. Loomis, even though he's in his eighties and his vision has been fading since the early aughts."

She made a slight grimace, grabbed the sugar container, and poured some into her tea. "They never make it sweet enough for me. Anyway, where was I?"

I was beginning to think I'd misjudged Char. She'd seemed to be relatively normal last night. But showing up late, ordering for me without asking my opinion, and her lack of focus made me wonder if I'd made a mistake.

"Oh yeah, no patients today. At least, none of the living variety. Since most of the folks in town avoid me, I'm forced to take on less savory tasks, like acting as the parish coroner."

Her words sank in. "Like handling dead people?" I didn't consider myself squeamish, but the thought of touching dead flesh always made me feel nauseated. "How did you get that gig?"

Char shrugged. "My brother's the sheriff, and he offered me the gig when the last coroner retired. There weren't exactly a ton of candidates, and he knew I could use the extra money until my clinic picks up. It's actually the reason I was late today."

My breath quickened. She'd come to lunch with me after inspecting a dead body. I fought back the bile that threatened to rise in my throat. Presley appearing saved me from having to say anything.

The pretty waitress set down two red plastic baskets filled with some kind of sandwich and a pile of what appeared to be homemade potato chips with some kind of orange seasoning.

Char dug into her basket with a passion. "Try it," she said between bites. "You've never had a sandwich like this. Trust me."

The sandwich was comprised of some kind of white bread, deli meats—all pork, sliced white cheese, and an oily slaw of some kind containing diced olives, celery, cauliflower, and carrots. The whole mess was covered in garlic and oregano.

Nothing about this combination made my mouth water, but the way Char was inhaling hers made me willing to take a chance on the unknown. I lifted the concoction to my mouth and took an exploratory bite.

Flavor like I'd never tasted exploded on my tongue.

"See?" Char said, her voice muffled by the bite she was currently chewing.

I swallowed, then tried one of the chips. The Cajun spices proved a nice complement to the Italian sandwich.

"Now if I can just get you to try sweet tea," Char said after she took another drink of hers.

I shook my head. "I have to draw the line at all that sugar. I mean, you're a doctor. You can't tell me that much sweetener is good for you."

"It might not be good for the body, but it's good for the soul."

We both laughed, and I realized that Char might not be normal, but normal had never been a requirement for my friendship before, and it made no sense to make it one now, especially in New Orleans.

I watched as she wiped her hands on a napkin, then leaned back in the booth, putting her hands on her stomach with a groan. "I love those things, but I always get too full, and then I want a nap."

I set the sandwich down, not even halfway through it. I couldn't afford a lethargic afternoon as I'd promised Luanne that I'd finish transferring the young adult fiction to the new shelves we'd recently had installed. "Thanks for the lunch suggestion. I never would have tried it if you hadn't forced my hand."

"Happy to do the dirty work," she said, then stared me in the face. "I hope you'll take this next part as easily as you accepted the lunch order."

Brow furrowed, I asked her what she meant.

Char leaned in and grabbed a hold of my hand. I thought it was odd until she spoke again. "We're trying to keep things real quiet for now. You know how quickly rumors can spread in a small town. I'm only telling you because it might have some bearing on the book club."

"What do you mean?" I asked, goosebumps breaking out across my skin.

"That dead body I mentioned? It's Tabby Means."

CHAPTER 4

I almost choked on the sip of water I'd just taken, and I grabbed a napkin and patted my face. I needed to recover from the shock of what I'd just learned.

Tabby. The mouthy blonde from last night. She's dead.

"Wait, did you say Tabby Means?"

Char nodded. "She's married to Vince Means, the richest man in town. Vince was married to Mercy before he dropped her for Tabby. Hence their little dialogue last night."

I nodded. It made sense, even if two women who hated each other passionately having the same name didn't.

Char kept her voice lowered, looking around to make certain we weren't overheard. "She was found this morning in one of the bays in Scar's garage, so someone at the book club meeting last night is potentially the last person to see her alive."

My eyes widened. "Do you know what happened yet?"

"The theory is suicide," Char replied. "There was a hose attached to her exhaust pipe that was pushed into the back window. The car could have idled until it ran out of gas. By that time, Tabby would have been stone cold."

I swallowed hard, pushing the basket of half-eaten food away from me. I could feel my stomach arguing with itself on whether to keep its contents or to reject them. A few deep breaths staved off the worst of my nausea, but I was still horrified.

"She doesn't seem like the suicide type," I whispered.

Char shrugged. "Suicide doesn't always have a *type*. I've done a rudimentary examination of the body, and so far, there doesn't look to be any other causes of death. No marks, bruises, or anything else that might signal foul play. But I sent some samples into the lab just to make certain. We'll have our answer soon."

"She was married to the richest man in town. She was beautiful. Those seem like some pretty heavy advantages. Why throw it all away?" I still couldn't believe that the fierce female from last night would turn around and take her own life.

Char sighed. "While New Orleans might seem like a charming southern town on the outside, it has its dirty little secrets. Especially when it comes to the town's most prominent figures." She jerked her thumb over her shoulder in the direction of City Hall, which was just visible in the distance from the diner's front windows. "Take the mayor, for example. It's an open secret that he's having an affair with his assistant."

I blinked, wondering how Dottie had let something like that slide when she was usually so eager to gossip about anything and everything tawdry in New Orleans.

"And when Tabby and Vince hooked up, it was nothing short of a scandal. The whole town was on edge, likely because the sugar refinery that Vince owns is New Orleans's biggest employer. Everyone thought Mercy would take Vince to the cleaners and he might have to sell the refinery, but it never happened. As you can see, Mercy's churning out jewelry to make ends meet while Tabby rides around like queen of the Parish."

Char finished off her sweet tea. "Well, she used to anyway. My point is, if you've been seeing our quaint little southern town through rose-colored glasses, it would be wise to trade them in for a magnifying glass. You won't have to look too deep to find the skeletons people around here are trying to bury."

My gaze unfocused and wandered the diner as I absorbed Char's words. When it hit on the clock over the door, I realized I was going to be late getting back from lunch. "I'm afraid I'm going to have to cut this conversation short," I said, the apology in my tone apparent. "I have to get back to the library."

"I hope I didn't scare you off," Char said, biting her lip.

I shook my head. "I'm not scared of you. It's the head librarian that puts the fear of God in me."

Char laughed. "Miss Luanne scares almost everyone in this town. Except maybe Scar's old pit bull. My brother says they're cousins."

It was my turn to laugh. "Thanks for sharing today."

Char nodded. "I thought you might need to know before our next book club meeting. I know the first one probably didn't go the way you'd planned, so I was hoping to save you from being blindsided a second time."

"I appreciate it. And thanks for the sandwich suggestion." I pulled out a couple bills to pay my share, but Char waved it away.

"It's on me this time. Least I can do for being late."

I thanked her, then pushed my way out the diner's door, hustling down the sidewalk to make it back to the library before Luanne noticed I was late. I should have known that luck wouldn't be on my side.

"Lunch breaks last one hour. No longer. No exceptions."

"Sorry," I mumbled as I passed her at the circulation desk. "It won't happen again."

"See that it doesn't." My boss fixed me with a heavy gaze. "Those youth fiction books are still waiting for your attention."

"I'll get them on the new shelves this afternoon."

Walking to the back of the library to grab a cart, I couldn't help but go over all I'd learned at lunch. Tabby Means was dead. I might not have known her hardly at all, but she was a member of my book club, and I already felt a little possessive over those members.

Moving to New Orleans gave me the opportunity to make an impact on a community, and though it may be small, it still meant a lot to me. Already, that community was one person smaller, and I felt the loss—if not for Tabby herself, as I'd barely met her, then for the town as a whole. And for my fledgling book club as well.

I grabbed a cart and wheeled it to the current Young Adult shelf, beginning to organize books for the move. Soon, I was pushing the cart to the new shelving unit, which could hold more books. Our budget was small, so I wasn't sure how long it would take to fill these shelves, but it gave me a hint of hope for the future to counter the grief of earlier.

Two days later, I was admiring my handiwork while I was reshelving the returned books. The new shelves were neatly organized, no title out of place. I was going back for a second load of returns when the library doors opened and in walked Stanley.

He had a stack of books in his hands, which he promptly dropped into the Returns slot that was built into the circulation desk. I waved to him, and he gave me a dopey smile and waved back, then wandered into the stacks.

I continued working for another half hour until all the recent returns were in their rightful places. I was coming back with another cartload of books when I passed the horror section and saw Stanley perusing its selection. He pulled out a book featuring a creepy-looking tree on the front.

I paused. "I read that one. It was good."

He glanced up at me and nodded.

Abandoning the cart, I approached, pulling another book off the shelf. "This one is by the same author, and it plays off the book you have in your hand. I'd suggest grabbing them both in case we have any dark and stormy nights in our future."

This earned me a chuckle. I noticed he was wearing a different T-shirt than before, but it featured the same character, the one with the devil and his lolling grin. Stanley took the book from my hand and added it to a small stack he'd set on the floor beside him.

He reminded me of myself, always tucking a book in my purse in case I had a few spare moments to read it. Or surrounding myself with stacks of unread books at home, eager to delve into new worlds and discover new favorite characters. "Is horror your favorite genre?"

Stanley shook his head and then shrugged. He seemed to be debating something as a series of emotions paraded across his face. At last, he spoke. "I don't know if I could say I have a favorite genre. To me, it's more about the story than the category we assign it."

"Well said," I replied, glad that I'd managed to make him open up again. Sally had given me the impression that silence was his natural state.

I wasn't about to waste the opportunity to chat with someone who did so little talking. Figuring that the shelves could wait, I dove into conversation with Stanley. It didn't take long to realize that he was extremely well read. I was so engrossed in our discussion that I didn't hear Luanne's footsteps as they approached.

I saw her as she turned the corner and prepared an excuse, but it turned out that she wasn't alone. The head librarian was flanked by two men in uniform with guns on their belts.

"Here he is," Luanne said before turning on her heel and walking away.

The men passed me by, making a beeline for Stanley. My jaw dropped as the shorter man pulled out a pair of handcuffs while the taller one began the Miranda recitation. "You have the right to remain silent."

How appropriate, I thought, slapping a hand over my mouth to keep from saying it out loud. I couldn't believe that Stanley was being arrested right in front of me, and it was clear the situation was overloading my brain.

"You have the right to an attorney. If you cannot afford an attorney, one will be appointed for you."

I couldn't hold back any longer. "What are you doing?"

The taller one looked me over like I was missing some marbles. "Arresting him for the murder of Tabitha Means."

It took me a moment to process the words I'd heard. Murder? Char had made it seem like suicide. I could see the fear in Stanley's eyes and it broke my heart. "You can't arrest him without evidence. What proof do you have?"

The taller one turned to his companion, his expression broadcasting that he wasn't thrilled with the question. "Take Taz down to the station and start processing him."

Before I could protest further, he turned back to me, blocking my view of Stanley and his escort.

"I don't believe we've met yet." His voice was like thick smoke. "I'm Sheriff Rains." His hands were on his belt, which meant there was no opportunity to shake one.

So this was the brother Char had mentioned. I could see the resemblance. He was taller than his sister and more muscular, but their eyes were the same, and his hair was a dark russet, not too far off from Char's auburn shade.

"Nice to meet you, Sheriff," I replied when it became clear he wasn't going to say anything else. "I'm Jade Hastings, the new assistant librarian, and I know this might get us started off on the wrong foot, but I think you have the wrong man."

He stared down at me, expressionless. "No offense, Miss Hastings, but you're new around here. There are plenty of things you don't yet understand about our little town."

"I might be new, but I've probably talked to that young man more than almost anybody in this town, so I'll say it again. You've got the wrong man. What is your evidence against Stanley?"

"I wasn't aware that you moonlighted as a defense attorney," he said. "But if you must know, Taz was the last one to see the deceased alive."

"That doesn't sound like much proof to hang a murder on," I countered. "Not to mention that I'd heard it was suicide, not murder."

The sheriff's eyes widened at the mention of suicide. I watched as he shook his head and muttered something about his sister running her mouth under his breath. "It might have looked like a suicide, but new evidence has come to light, evidence that indicates foul play. Someone murdered Tabby Means, and since Taz was the last one seen with her and because he's generally considered to be the town weirdo, I'm pretty confident that we got the right guy."

Sheriff Rains turned to go, but I followed, not willing to let this go. "The town weirdo? That's your evidence? From what I've seen,

Stanley is gentle, well read, and well spoken. He's just quiet and awkward, but that doesn't make him a killer."

The sheriff showed no interest as he crossed the library in a determined stride that had me jogging to keep up. I wasn't willing to let the matter go, though. I hadn't known Stanley for very long, but it was clear to me that he couldn't have committed a crime like the one he'd been arrested for.

"Tabby gave him a lift home after our book club meeting," I said. "That's why they were together that night, not for some nefarious purpose."

Rains stopped suddenly, causing me to bounce into his back and nearly lose my footing. His expression was one of annoyance. "That might be true, but it doesn't explain why Pops Parker saw them together. If Tabby was just dropping Taz off at home, they wouldn't have been speeding past Pop's gas station, which is well past the turnoff to Taz's house. So I'm afraid your explanation doesn't hold water, Miss Hastings."

He started off again, and I followed, my stomach knotting. I was used to the well-ordered world of the library where everything made sense. Suddenly, nothing made sense. "Sheriff, he wouldn't do this. My gut is telling me that you have the wrong man."

The sheriff had reached the doors, but he paused, looking back at me. "This wouldn't be the first time someone's gut has been wrong." He nodded to Luanne, who was watching the scene unfold from behind the circulation desk. "Thanks for your help, Miss Luanne."

"Anytime," she replied with a perfunctory nod.

The sheriff gave me one last look and departed without another word.

I barely restrained myself from throwing up my hands in frustration and letting out a choice string of curses. I watched the sheriff as he walked away, thinking that the friendliness gene must have skipped one of the Rains children.

"The book club is canceled," Luanne said, making me turn around and face her with a look of confusion on my face.

"I'm sorry?"

"I'm not having that group meeting in my library, after hours no less. It seems the only thing that club attracts is degenerates." She went back to scanning the returned books into the computer system, the law having been laid down.

I took a moment to catch my breath, then headed back to the book cart I'd abandoned to talk to Stanley.

My book club had lasted exactly one week. I'd set out hoping to contribute to the community, but all I'd created was an apparent preamble for a murder.

"No," I mumbled to myself. I wasn't willing to give up so easily. Not on the book club and not on clearing Stanley's name. Char had said this town had buried secrets.

Maybe it was time to start digging them up.

CHAPTER 5

Nerves were turning my stomach upside down, but I did my best to ignore them as I uncorked a bottle of wine and straightened up the fruit plate I'd set out. A black and white ball of fur hopped onto the coffee table and I hurried to shoo him away from the cheese and cracker plate.

"Go on, Chonks. You're fat enough as it is."

His tail swished around in disagreement, but he jumped down, only to circle around twice and collapse on the rug, lifting his leg to lick his privates.

"Chonks! We're about to have company!"

I gave up on trying to teach my cat manners when the doorbell rang. Mentally crossing my fingers, I made my way down the hall to the wide front door and opened it. Char stood on the porch, a copy of a book under her arm.

"Hey, girl," she said, giving me a hug. I was getting used to hugging as a form of greeting since the move. As she entered, Char looked around and let out a long whistle. "This place is massive."

I shrugged. "Uncle Mike loved history. I think that's why he moved down here."

"He must have been 'rich Uncle Mike.' This much history doesn't come cheap."

I chuckled at her observation. "I really didn't know him that well. He wrote a letter and included it with his will, saying that I was the only member of the family that would appreciate the library he'd built, so he was giving it to me, along with the building that held it. Which just happened to be this old plantation house."

We headed down the hall, and I led her through the open double doors into the library. To me and Uncle Mike, it was the crowning glory of the house. Others might crow about the grand staircase, the colonnaded walkway wrapped in vines in the garden, or even the intricate molding, but for a librarian like me, nothing could beat the library for not only its design but also its contents.

There were more than a couple first editions under glass in the cases beneath the windows, and the busts on the mantle above the big stone fireplace were of famous authors like Dante, Shakespeare, and Milton. The rest of the walls held floor-to-ceiling shelves, each full to the brim with books.

A wrought-iron spiral staircase led to a second-floor balcony that ran the length and width of the room, and shelves lined those walls as well. It was like something out of a magazine with the title *Luxurious Libraries of the Filthy Rich.* The furniture was made of brown leather, and there were more than enough seats for the club members.

"God Lord Baby Jesus," Char breathed, her hand on her chest. "Don't ever bring Miss Luanne here. She might keel over dead in front of the fireplace from envy."

"I don't think we need to worry about Luanne coming anywhere near here. I think she'd rather chew nails."

"Nah, she does that for fun," Char replied. We both laughed, but the pitch of Char's laugh suddenly rose. "And who do we have here?"

Chonks was weaving between her legs, rubbing himself against her and purring in greeting.

"That's Sir Chonksworth the Bold, or Chonks for short."

"Well, isn't that a mouthful?" Char said, squatting down to pet his head. "But you look regal enough to deserve that moniker." She gave him another few strokes, then sneezed twice. "Well, I may be a little allergic."

The doorball rang again, and I left Char with Chonks, asking her to keep an eye on the cheese. It was Sally, who greeted me with another hug. I led her into the library, where Chonks sniffed at her before butting his head into her shin.

I thought this was a good opportunity to talk about what had happened at the public library. "Have you talked to Stanley since his arrest?"

Sally frowned. "I visited him at the jail, but he wouldn't say anything to me. He just sat there, head down, eyes staring at his hands."

"Poor boy," Char said. "I can't believe my brother thinks he did this."

"He was the last person seen with Tabby that night," I said. "Apparently, someone named Pops saw them drive past his establishment."

"I don't know why that would be," Sally said. "Stanley lives almost a mile before the gas station. Why would he still be in the car when Tabby drove past Pop's place?" She scowled. "Pop has to be a hundred years old by now. Maybe he couldn't see properly."

"That can't be the only piece of evidence," Char said. "My brother might be a pain in my behind, but he's not stupid, and he would know Pop's ID wouldn't be enough to hang a conviction on."

"What other evidence could there be?" I asked.

Char's shoulders lifted. "I don't know. He's being tight lipped since he found out I told you about Tabby before he wanted it to get out."

"Since all this went down after the last book club meeting, maybe tonight we'll be able to turn up some clue of who could have really done this heinous act. I don't believe Stanley could have."

Sally nodded her agreement. "Stanley might have some problems, but he's a sweet boy who has never done an unkind thing in his life. I don't care if they have video of him at the scene holding a sign that says, 'I did it.' I still wouldn't believe it."

I patted her on the shoulder and headed back to the front door when the doorbell rang again. The rest of the group trickled in over the next few minutes, and soon, we were all seated in the library. Chonks made sure to grab as much attention as he could. Although he turned up his nose at a couple group members, he climbed all over others.

I could only shrug and apologize for my cat's rudeness. "He thinks he's in charge."

Chonks looked at me with an expression that said, "And you don't?"

I picked him up, holding him in my lap as I called the meeting to order. I'd put some thought into how to start things off this week, but as I looked around at the women's faces, the words stuck in my throat. Nothing seemed appropriate, neither mentioning what had happened or ignoring it. So I stuck to what I knew: books.

"*The Great Gatsby* was written at a time of upheaval in an America that was facing a crisis of identity. Its struggles with morality, with excess and deprivation, are the backdrop against which our story unfolds."

"It sounds like New Orleans today," Alma said in what sounded like an attempted whisper to Dinah, who was seated next to her, but was loud enough to be heard by the whole group.

"Doesn't it just?" Dottie asked.

And just like that, I lost control of the conversation.

"It's just awful what happened to Tabby Means, isn't it?" the elderly gossip said, her gloved hands folded neatly in her lap.

There were a few murmured words of agreement, and at the same time, I heard Mercy grumble that "awful" wasn't the word she'd use to describe it.

I tried to regain some semblance of order, but the women were talking over one another and paying me no attention. Chonks hopped down from my lap and padded across the floor, his fluffy tail like a flag announcing his departure.

"What I want to know is, were Taz and Tabby having an affair?" The question from Mercy caused everyone to quiet down.

"Everyone knows there's something wrong with that boy," Alma said with a sniff.

Sally was quick to defend her employee. "That's not true! Stanley is a good boy. He's always on time to work, always helpful, never rude or angry."

"It's always the quiet ones," Dottie said softly.

"They found her in Scar's garage, right?" Mercy unconsciously tugged at the gaudy necklace around her neck, undoubtedly one of her own designs. "Why would Taz take her there?"

"If it wasn't Taz, someone else could have lured her there," Char said.

"Tabby used to be hot and heavy with the boy who works there, Jimmy Beal. His father had a heart attack in that hooker's bed, remember?"

Alma shook her head at Dottie's tidbit, holding a lace handkerchief up to her nose. "No reason to be crass, Miss Dottie."

"She's right, though," Sally said. "Jimmy and Tabby used to date. Maybe this was his way of getting back at her for breaking up with him."

Jimmy Beal sounded like a solid lead. He worked at the garage and he had a history with Tabby. So why didn't Sheriff Rains arrest Jimmy? Why was he pinning this on Stanley?

I reached for the wine bottle, but it was as empty as my glass, so I stood and headed for the kitchen to retrieve another. I pulled it out of the cupboard, glad that I could at least serve alcohol this week since we were no longer at the library.

I turned with the bottle in my hand and almost dropped it in surprise when I saw Dinah standing in the kitchen, inspecting the molding that decorated the ceiling. I hadn't heard her approach, despite how squeaky the floors in the hallway were.

"This molding looks original," she said brightly. "It could use some TLC though." The older woman looked at me, a polite grin on her face. "So could the rest of the place. Did you know you had a loose step on your front porch? And I noticed a few nails coming out of the hardwood boards in the parlor as I came in. The baseboard in the sitting room is pulling away from the wall as well."

I kept my expression neutral, but my body was stiff. I wondered when she'd had time to catalogue the deficiencies in the old plantation house. I spent most of my time in the library, so maybe I hadn't paid much attention to the condition of some of the rooms. There were too many of them to keep up with anyway.

"It's a shame to have such a lovely property and not keep up with it," she said, her tone imitating that of a friend with some needed advice. But I hadn't solicited any advice, and something about Dinah rubbed me the wrong way. Still, she continued, failing to pick up on my body language. "Someone could be hurt, and you could end up with a lawsuit on your hands. Not somewhere you'd like to be."

I opened my mouth to suggest we rejoin the group, but she put a hand on my arm and leaned in, her tone sweeter than cane sugar. "This might be too much house for someone your age, sweetheart. Have you ever considered selling? You could buy yourself a cute little bungalow and end up with a nice nest egg."

"I'm not really interested—"

"It's important to preserve our history, you know," she said, her grip tightening slightly and her eyes going glassy. "This place could be a real jewel in the right hands."

"It certainly could," I said, choosing the path of least resistance. "Now, let's get back to the others. I'm sure they're pretty thirsty by now."

I pushed past Dinah but waited at the doorway to make sure she followed me. Back in the library, the group was still chattering away. Public opinion seemed to be split. Some thought it was Stanley, or Taz as most called him, on account of his favorite shirt. A couple others thought it unlikely that Stanley had it in him.

I felt a little better knowing that others shared my doubts. Still, I realized I wasn't going to get anywhere with the book club ladies in a group like this. There were too many distractions. I decided that I'd do my investigating one on one from now on.

I'd never really been a fan of mysteries, preferring instead plots that didn't try to cheat readers with false fronts and dead ends. And now that I was living inside one of those darn books, I couldn't say that my opinion had changed.

Maybe I could change the narrative, though. Turn it into a story of redemption.

That was better than the tragedy it seemed destined to become.

CHAPTER 6

I was the only customer in the Tip Top Grocery that morning, meaning Sally had time to continue our conversation about what had really happened to Tabby Means.

"I still can't believe this is happening," Sally said, shaking her head while stacking cans of tomato paste onto a shelf, a job I was certain Stanley used to help her with. "How anyone could think he could do such a thing is beyond me."

"You mentioned someone named Jimmy Beal at the last book club meeting. You said maybe he was looking for some kind of revenge against Tabby?"

Sally paused in her shelf stocking. "Jimmy is a local boy who went to high school with Tabby. They used to run around together a lot in her beauty pageant days. He suited her much better than Vince in my opinion."

"Why do you say that?"

"Well, because they were the same kind. You know? Trailer trash." She'd leaned in to whisper those last two words.

I nodded. "And Vince is wealthy."

Sally laughed. "That's putting it mildly. His refinery employs most of the town. His family has been in New Orleans for ages, and their influence stretches back generations. Although he might be a philanderer, Vince still comes from wholesome southern stock, or some people might say."

The pieces of the puzzle were getting closer together, but I knew I still wasn't close to putting the edges of the thing together, let alone the puzzle's innards. "Does Jimmy seem like the type of person who could do this?"

Shrugging, Sally resumed her stocking. "He's had a couple run-ins with the law, but nothing too serious. He likes to drink and get rowdy sometimes, not unlike several other gentleman of New Orleans, Louisiana."

"If Jimmy is a better suspect, I wonder why the sheriff didn't haul him in." Without a better idea of the evidence against Stanley, I couldn't be sure of why Rains had zeroed so conclusively in on the poor boy.

"I wish I could tell you." Sally let out a little huff. "But Jimmy isn't the only person I'd put on my suspect list. Tabby wasn't exactly well liked around here. There are plenty of people who are probably privately rejoicing that she's no longer around to act all high and mighty. Folks used to say that she thought her *Miss Bon Temps* crown was real so she acted like royalty, but a wealthy husband and a plastic crown couldn't make people like her when she acted like she owned the place."

"So Jimmy isn't the only person with an ax to grind?"

"No ma'am. I don't think her own husband even liked her anymore. And we already know Mercy hated her guts, and with good reason. Then there is anyone else who Tabby talked down to, offended, or treated like dirt. Throw a rock in New Orleans, and you're bound to hit someone Tabby ticked off."

It sounded like I had my work cut out for me. It would be tough to narrow down a list of suspects if everyone had a reason to hate Tabby Means. This just reinforced my need to find out what evidence Rains had against Stanley. I had to understand what I was up against.

"Do you have any more of those pastries? The ones with the powdered sugar on top?" I'd picked up a couple last week and I'd been craving more ever since.

"The beignets? Sure, I think I have a few more." Sally straightened and headed to the small glass case that held an assortment of baked goods. "I'll give you all I got left."

I watched as she loaded a small brown paper bag with the tasty treats. "I'm gonna go down to the sheriff's office again," she said. "Gonna see if I can bring Stanley a few things to eat that aren't canned baked beans and Wonder Bread. That jail food is atrocious."

"That's very nice of you," I said as she passed me the bag. "What do I owe you?"

"Girl, you can just take those off my hands for nothing. If they stick around too long, they end up in my belly." Sally put her hands on her stomach, which was flat as could be.

"Well, I appreciate the sentiment, but now they're going to go in my belly where they will join the ghosts of the others I've taken down." I would be as fat as Chonks soon if I didn't stop pigging out on southern cuisine.

Sally chuckled. "I think your figure can take it. Men like girls with meat on their bones."

I held back an eye roll at her comment. Men were the last thing on my mind. I'd had a couple run-ins with the opposite sex in my day, but I'd never found one worth keeping around. At least with a good book, you could reread and be transported into a world of wonder. The only place a man had ever transported me was a Captain Larry's Bar and Grill, and I'd had to pay for my own Mermaid's Delight.

"Thanks for the pastries and the chat," I said, waving as I headed out the door.

It was another sultry spring day, and I wondered how I was going to survive the heat of the summer. Maybe this was where Baum had gotten the idea for the Wicked Witch melting in the Wizard of Oz. The humidity certainly made me want to collapse into a puddle.

Char's clinic was close, which meant that my car's air conditioning hadn't wrestled the warmth to a standstill yet, so I'd rolled down the windows. My hair now resembled a bird's nest that had been condemned by the bird city council.

I tried to tame it as I rushed toward the entrance, in need of the sweet relief of conditioned air. Relieved that the waiting room was empty, I ducked into the restroom and managed to comb my hair out to something a little less ragged in the mirror.

When I returned to the waiting room, Char was just coming out of the entrance to examination rooms with an older man dressed in a white undershirt and a pair of overalls he filled to overflowing.

"You didn't hit the tuning fork and hold it to the bottom of my feet," he said. "Dr. Loomis does that every time."

I could tell by the look on Char's face that she was exercising extreme patience. "I told you last time, Lou, that I don't have to do the tuning fork at every exam. You weren't coming in today for your diabetes. We were looking at that rash on your back. Your feet have nothing to do with it."

"You gonna complain about my sugars now? Dr. Loomis said I can have sugar in my coffee as long as I stay active."

"Lou, I didn't bring up your sugars, but since you did, I don't think Dr. Loomis knew you drank a gallon of coffee a day and took two spoonfuls of sugar in every cup. You need to cut down or consider artificial sweeteners if you really can't give it up."

"Damnation, doctor. You'll be the death of me. Dr. Loomis said—"

Char's restraint finally broke. "Dr. Rains says that you can take yourself back to Dr. Loomis if you don't like the way I practice medicine. Now kindly haul yourself home. I've got another patient."

Lou turned his squinty eyes in my direction and let out a snuff of air. "She's ornery as a pig with an empty trough." The man shook his head and made an exit at last.

Char heaved an enormous sigh and threw herself into a chair, putting her hand to her forehead in dramatic fashion. "My trough is empty. But I can smell Miss Sally's beignets, and they're sure to cure my orneriness."

I laughed and tossed her the bags of pastries. "Rough day?"

"I really shouldn't complain," she said between bites of beignets. "I'm grateful for every patient at this point. Except Lou. That man could drive me to abandon medicine and work in a Waffle House."

She dusted the powdered sugar off her white coat and thanked me. "Lou was right. I really needed that dose of fat and sugar."

Shaking my head, I sat down beside her. "Sally and I were talking about possible suspects, since we both believe Stanley didn't do it."

Char nodded. "You haven't been here long, Jade. What makes you so certain Taz didn't kill Tabby?"

I leaned back, eyes wide. "You think he did?"

Char's face was neutral. "My brother does, and I tend to trust his judgment."

"He couldn't have. He's shy, bright, and harmless. I saw him carry a spider outside so it wouldn't be harmed, a spider I would have killed without a second thought. It just doesn't add up."

Her neutrality crumbled. "I know," she said, throwing up her hands. "I tried to tell Charlie he was wrong, but he ignored me, instead chewing me a new one for telling you about Tabby when he told me to keep it quiet."

"Sorry," I said, biting my lip and snagging a beignet from the bag before Char inhaled them all.

She shrugged. "I don't blame you. It's just that he told me to keep my mouth shut about the results of the tox screen too, and I knew I'd end up spilling the beans. I don't think Taz did it either."

At last, hard evidence. "What did the tox screen find?"

"It wasn't suicide, unless Tabby somehow got her hands on a lethal dose of benzodiazepine. She doesn't have a prescription. We checked with Mercer."

"Could she have taken some pills and gone the carbon monoxide route? A double dose, just to make sure the job was done?" Those might have been the most brutal questions I had ever uttered.

Char's brow furrowed. "It wasn't pills. It was liquid and very fast acting. And there's no way she could have done both. The cause of death was an overdose, not carbon monoxide poisoning. She was already dead by the time her car was parked in the garage."

I swallowed hard. "It really was murder."

Char nodded, staring down at the floor. "And the killer tried to make it look like a suicide by staging her in the garage."

"The murderer must have chosen that location with a reason in mind," I said. "He wanted people to think she'd killed herself where her ex-boyfriend would find her."

"The killer had to make her suicide plausible so Charlie wouldn't investigate, but then he found Taz's shirt at the scene," Char said.

"Making it look like Taz—er, Stanley had something to do with it."

"And his prints were all over the car."

"Yes, but Tabby was giving him a ride home, so of course they would be." I ran my hands through my hair, realizing I'd probably just fluffed it up again. "It doesn't make sense. Your brother thinks Stanley somehow overdosed Tabby then staged a suicide. He went through all of that trouble just to leave his T-shirt behind?"

"And where did Taz get that much benzodiazepine? He'd never get a prescription for that amount." Char pursed her lips, her face filled with confusion.

"I still keep coming back to the question of motive. It seems like half the town has a better motive for killing Tabby than Taz does."

An unnamed emotion flittered across Char's face before she shut it down, but I still caught it.

"What is it?" I asked. "Would Taz have a motive?"

Char frowned. "They went to school together. Our Lady of Perpetual Help. That's where everyone around here went, me included. But I was gone by the time of Tabby's heyday."

"Let me guess. She wasn't the shy, retiring type in high school?"

"She was not." Char dug the last beignet out of the bag. "She was a bully, and there were plenty of reasons to pick on a boy like Taz."

"Could something have happened back then to—"

The door opened and I froze mid-sentence as the most attractive male I'd seen in the flesh entered the clinic, one of his hands holding the other, which was wrapped in a paper towel.

My heart beat faster. Maybe I'd been premature to write off the appeal of the opposite sex. *Please let him have a slow southern drawl and still open doors for ladies and call his mother every week.*

And please, don't let him be allergic to cats.

CHAPTER 7

"Ethan," Char said, coming to her feet. "I thought I just sewed that hand back on."

The handsome man chuckled. "Sorry, boss. I told you I'd be better off with a robot hand but you said organic is better than inorganic."

"That does sound like me." Char turned to me. "Jade, this is Ethan Millbank, handyman extraordinaire."

"Hi," I said, restraining myself as I got hold of my imagination. It was clear my hormones weren't as dormant as I'd thought.

"Nice to meet you," he said. "I'd offer to shake your hand, but I cut myself on a rusty nail, which is why I'm here." Ethan addressed Char, one corner of his mouth coming up in a lopsided grin. "What do you say, Doc? Once more into the breach for old times' sake?"

"Follow me," Char said, leading him into the back. She gave me a wave. "I'll see you at the funeral."

"Not if I see you first."

Ethan looked at me a little strangely, and I realized how inappropriate that might sound after Char's mention of a funeral. Blushing red until my skin was the same shade as a Halloween demon, I rushed out the clinic's door, berating myself for my idiocy.

So much for Ethan, I told myself as I jogged to my car before I wilted. I slid behind the wheel, glanced in the rearview mirror, and blanched. If my corniness didn't scare him away, my hair definitely had.

Giving up, I rolled down the windows and started the car, heading toward Mercer's pharmacy. I didn't know if I'd be able to get any information out of Patrick Mercer, but he'd seemed friendly enough when I'd stopped in for tape. If anyone would know about where a person could get a lot of liquid benzodiazepine, a pharmacist should.

I was grateful that the drug store was empty because at this point, I was afraid my hairstyle would frighten small children and dogs. Luckily, Mercer's Drug was a cavalcade of odds and ends, a cavalcade that included a hat rack littered with ball caps with silly phrases. I grabbed one with a fish in lipstick on it and shoved it over my head just before Patrick came out from behind his pharmacy counter to greet me.

"Out of tape already?" he asked with an affable smile.

"Thankfully no. I just came in for something to keep the sun out of my eyes." I pointed at the cap.

I'd expected the odd look he gave me and laughed, saying I collected joke hats. That made him chuckle, and he spent a couple minutes pointing out some choice caps, telling me how seriously he'd taken the ordering process, which seemed to consist of him opening a light beer and paging through the catalog while reading the sayings on the hats to his dog.

"Bubbles has a wonderful sense of humor."

As he adjusted his glasses, I tried to think of a way to turn the conversation to the Means murder. "Humor is so important, especially in such tragic times."

Patrick blinked. It was clear he wasn't certain what I referring to.

"Her funeral is coming up," I continued. "I bet half the town will be there, dressed in black."

"You mean the Means girl," he said, his voice low. "If I know Vince, the funeral—if there is one—will be private."

I was surprised by his response. "The newspaper said she'd be laid to rest tomorrow." There'd been no mention of a private ceremony.

Patrick took off his glasses and began methodically cleaning them with a thin cloth. "I never knew Tabby well, but I've had more than a few run-ins with her mother. There's no way Tammy Carter is going to miss an opportunity for some kind of dramatic display if Vince has a public funeral. Vince will want to head that off."

It appeared that bad blood existed between Tabby's mother and her husband. I filed that information away for later. Lowering my voice to take on a conspiratorial tone, I said, "I'd heard rumors that it was suicide, but now someone has been arrested. I thought I'd left murder behind in Baltimore."

He didn't answer for a moment, just slowly cleaned his glasses. I thought maybe I'd offended him, but he finally replaced his glasses back on his face and spoke. "It's a shame, but just because we're not a big city doesn't mean we don't have our share of crime. It wouldn't be the first time, and I doubt it will be the last."

His words gave me a chill, turning the sweat on my brow cold. "They said he gave her something to knock her out. Any idea where he could have gotten something like that?"

His mouth flattened into a line. "Just what are you suggesting, young lady?"

I straightened and held up my hands, palms up. "I'm sorry, Patrick. I didn't mean to offend you." I laughed nervously. "I'll level with you. I'm a big Agatha Christie fan, and now it's like I've walked into one of her novels. I got a little carried away."

Patrick's expression loosened but only slightly. "I'll tell you what I told Sheriff Rains. He didn't get it from me."

"I never thought he did," I said, my tone softening. "I assumed it was something someone could get on the internet."

"Not without a prescription, not the pure stuff. You could get knockoffs from Southeast Asia, sure, but not the legitimate drug."

"So the person responsible would have to have a prescription?"

"The amount you'd need to overdose means it would have to be a very concentrated, large dose. I don't know anyone who would prescribe that much to one person. With a quantity like that, it most likely would have been taken from a supply more suited to a hospital or sleep disorder clinic." His words were matter of fact as he straightened the hats on display.

Although it was clear he wasn't happy with the topic, he was providing me with a lot of much-needed information.

I decided to press a little more. "You've lived here a long time, right?"

He nodded perfunctorily. "All my life."

"Is there any reason you can think of that Stanley might have wanted to kill Tabby?"

"I don't know why any sane person would want to kill anyone," he said in a huff. "Now, if you'll excuse me, I've got to get back to work." He abandoned the hat rack and strode back down the aisle.

"Wait! I have to pay for this cap."

"On the house," he said without even turning around.

It looked like I'd won the freebie lottery today. First the pastries and now a hideous hat.

"Thanks, Patrick," I said, wondering if I'd permanently burnt a bridge with the pharmacist.

I let myself back out onto the sweltering sidewalk, this time not bothering to run back to my car. I would have to accept this liquid heaviness that made it feel like you were swimming rather than walking. I reached my car, leaning against it to have a look at the state of downtown New Orleans on a Friday afternoon.

Before I could take in my surroundings, my bare arm touched the metal of my car and I let out a screech of pain at the burning sensation that followed. Calling myself nine kinds of moron, I unlocked my car and climbed inside. I turned the key, cranked up the air, and started for home.

Chonks was there waiting for me. I expected the usual dance that took place no matter what time I came home. He'd paw at my legs, complaining loudly about the state of his food bowl. For as big as that cat was, you would think he had never had a meal in his life from the way he carried on.

However, the joke cap seemed to put him off. He eyed the hat and ran off down the hallway, his tail swishing madly. I sighed, too tired to try and figure out what his deal was. I hurried to my sanctuary, shutting the library doors behind me and hitting the fan setting on the air conditioning. Soon, the room was as cool as a refreshing cocktail.

I didn't bother sitting down, knowing that Chonks would be scratching at the door soon enough. Less than a minute later, I heard his indignant cry in the hall and let him in, closing the door behind him to keep the air concentrated in the library. I collapsed onto the soft leather sofa, and Chonks followed, jumping up onto my stomach and proceeding to make biscuits out of my shirt.

I must have fallen asleep because the next thing I noticed was the insistent buzz of the doorbell. The shadows had lengthened in the library, and it was clearly a couple hours later than it had been when I'd settled onto the sofa.

I hopped up, still groggy, and hurried to the front door. Char was on the porch, a big paper bag in her arms. "Hey girl. Figured I'd pay you back for the beignets. How about some Thai food?"

"Thai food? In New Orleans?"

She laughed, walking inside. "Actually, it's from a client. She's an immigrant from Thailand and one of the only clients that doesn't compare me to Dr. Loomis. The only problem is, she pays her bills mostly in sticky rice and spring rolls, which isn't a currency most of my creditors accept. But it does help keep my belly full."

I was beginning to realize that Char's stomach called the shots, but I couldn't get mad. The Thai food smelled too good. Waving her in, we made our way to the kitchen.

Char emptied the bag of the containers it held while I pulled down a couple plates. Before long, we were both sighing in delight over the food we were ingesting.

"I miss Thai food," I said. "That and being able to get something hot to eat after nine PM."

Char laughed. "Yeah, after Sparky's closes, you're pretty much dependent on your own culinary skills. But that's the charm of a small town, right? No night life, no exotic restaurants, and a pharmacy that follows bank hours."

"Speaking of the pharmacy, I had an interesting chat with Patrick Mercer today." I set down my fork and leaned back in my chair before relating the details of my awkward conversation.

Char started coughing on her curry when I mentioned my Agatha Christie cover story. I couldn't tell if it was surprise at my genius or laughter at my folly that made her choke. Then I told her what Mercer had said about the funeral.

"I hadn't thought of that," she said, wiping at her mouth with a napkin. "He could be right. Tammy does like to make a fuss over anything she can, and Vince generally doesn't appreciate her hollering."

"A private funeral," I mused. "It's like they're trying to put a lid over this thing as tightly and as quickly as they can. Arrest a suspect, one that will never speak out because he generally doesn't speak at all. Then sweep everything under the rug before anyone realizes the truth."

Char frowned. "I hope the 'they' you're talking about doesn't include my brother. He's a good sheriff and a good man. Charlie is working with the evidence he has, which is probably a lot more than we have. Right now, all we've got amounts to a bunch of speculation and some good old-fashioned gossip."

"You're right," I said. "It's time to get serious about evidence. I made an appointment for an oil change at the garage where they found Tabby's body. And I'm going to figure out a way to talk to Vince, to see if he had anything to do with this."

Char let out a whistle at my ambition. "Good luck getting old Vince Means to sit down for a little chat. When he's in the office, he's busy. And when he's out of the office, he's not the type that likes to be disturbed."

"Well, I don't like the New Orleans Book Club being disturbed either. If I'm smart about things, he won't even realize that I'm looking into his wife's death."

"Okay, Miss Marple," she replied, nodding. "Let me know how I can help."

"Figuring out where the drugs Tabby overdosed on came from

would help."

Char cocked an eyebrow. "Boy, you don't ask for much, do you?"

"You're the coroner. I imagine you work pretty closely with the local authorities. Maybe you can push your contacts, see if you can convince someone to share what they know."

Char stood, crossing to the sink to rinse off her dish. "I can't promise anything, but I'll do my best. Charlie is playing things real close to the vest. Maybe he has his own suspicions about this thing being too tidy."

I was escorting her back to the front door when Chonks accosted us, lying down right in front of our path. Char giggled and leaned down to pet him, but before she could reach his fur, she let out a huge sneeze, causing him to give her an indignant look before racing from the room.

We both laughed, even though I said it was unkind to laugh at someone crazy, even if they're a cat. Chonks let out a meow from the windowsill where he'd fled to safety, almost as if he was complaining about what I'd said.

"I'll let you know if I get anywhere on Vince," I said. "Maybe I'll hit some good luck and—*oof*!"

The loose board Dinah had pointed out caught on the end of my bare foot and I tumbled to the floor, getting the air knocked out of me. I was fortunate to be in the company of a doctor, who immediately took a look at my foot.

"You'll live," she pronounced. "Although another fall like that could be worse. I suggest you give Ethan a call." She pulled out her phone and texted me his number. "He'll get it fixed up fast and won't charge you an arm and a leg. Although he might ask for two legs in your case, since the one is now damaged."

I hustled her out the door, laughing sarcastically at her joke. Shutting it behind her, I leaned against the door and looked at my phone where the handsome handyman's number was staring back at me.

Being taken out by an avoidable injury wouldn't help my investigation. That was just pure logic. No one could accuse me of any inappropriate motives.

I'll call him tomorrow. Strictly for business and not because I want to see his muscles flex in his plaid shirt while he works.

CHAPTER 8

The doorbell caught me off guard, and I managed to spill some of the hot tea I was making on my hand. Shaking my head at my accident-prone nature, I hustled to the door, this time aware of who stood on the other side.

It was two in the afternoon and Ethan was right on time. He greeted me with his lopsided smile, saying he'd already found a loose step on his way up to the porch. "Old houses like this always have some bumps and bruises, but it's not hard to fix things up if you have good bones."

"Thanks for coming out on short notice," I said, already getting flustered by his attractiveness and unable to come up with a play on "good bones" that didn't sound either morbid or sexually inappropriate.

"There isn't much else to do on a Thursday afternoon in New Orleans when it isn't football season," he replied. "It's either this or trying to pull some fish out of the river."

"I guess you weren't one of those invited to Tabby's funeral." The words just came out since we were mentioning alternate activities taking place today. I hadn't considered Ethan in connection to the crime at all.

He paused, puzzled for a moment. "No, I guess not. We weren't very close."

Feeling like an ass, I figured it was better to show him the needed repairs before I choked on my foot any further. Pointing out the loose board where I'd tripped last night, I started listing a few other places where the boards were coming up.

Chonks strolled down the hall like he'd built the place, standing directly in Ethan's way.

"Who is this prince?" Ethan asked, scratching the butterball behind the ears.

"You're making the acquaintance of Sir Chonksworth the Bold, first of his name. Long may he reign."

"Well, aren't you someone special?" he murmured when Chonks threw himself to the floor for better pets.

"He certainly thinks he is," I said, crossing my arms over my chest. "Feel free to move him along when he gets in your way. He thinks he knows better than everyone."

"He probably does," Ethan replied, his pitch rising an octave. "Don't you, Chonky-boy? How about I make you my assistant?"

His interaction with my cat was adorable, pushing my attraction to near crush levels.

"I guess I will leave you boys to it then." I positioned myself in the sitting room with a book at first so I could steal glances at him while he fixed the loose board. When he moved to the flooring in the second-floor hall, I pretended to dust the empty bedroom across from where he was working.

Back in the parlor, I organized the knick-knacks while he took care of the nails coming out of the floor. I thought he might get suspicious, but he seemed engrossed in conversation with his newly appointed assistant.

"You see, Chonky-boy, if you just hammer these back in, it's only a matter of time before they pop up again." He pulled out his drill, holding it up in front of Chonks, who, for his part, looked interested. "You have to replace the nails with screws and use a dab of this wood filler here to make sure they stick in the same holes."

Chonks didn't mind people, but there were very few he was this enthusiastic about. It seemed in the case of Ethan, we were on the same page.

I finally retreated to the kitchen, fanning myself—but for once not because of the heat. When I heard Ethan head out onto the porch, I made up two glasses of lemonade and took them out the front door. He was working on the loose step, so I set the glass of lemonade on the railing and took a seat in one of the old rocking chairs to drink my own glass.

"This is the last thing on the list," he said as he finished fixing the step. "All the issues were minimal repairs, and I had the materials I needed with me."

"I'm glad they are all so easily fixed."

I could hear scratching at the door and I shook my head. Chonks never scratched at the door. He was an indoor cat and he seemed to have made his peace with that fact. Sure, there was the one incident with the neighbor cat, but other than that, Chonks had accepted his fate.

"He must really be into you," I said, jerking my thumb at the door. *Just like his owner.*

"That makes two of us." Ethan straightened, putting a hammer back into his toolbelt which hung from his lean hips. "I love cats, but I haven't brought home another one since Buster died. He was a big orange barn cat and my best buddy. He left some big shoes to fill."

I was beginning to think the entry under "perfect" in the dictionary would need to include the phrase "see also: Ethan Millbank."

Ethan climbed back onto the porch and took a long drink from his glass of lemonade. "So how are you liking our little town?"

"It's different, but it's growing on me. Have you been in New Orleans long?"

"Just since I was born. I couldn't imagine living anywhere else. Which is why I go around fixing up old houses like these every day. I want to preserve the beauty of this place, keep it alive for future generations."

"It's nice to have a career you find rewarding," I said. "Like me and the library. My love of books makes the job enjoyable, and I get to share my passion with members of the community."

I realized how that could have sounded right after I said it, but thankfully, Ethan didn't seem to notice. "My passion is these old houses. I've studied types of antebellum architecture, the historical materials they used, and the building techniques the people of New Orleans used to employ. My specialization keeps me pretty busy around here, as these old places are always a little temperamental."

"You're not the only one who is enthusiastic about old houses," I said. "For instance, Dinah Mercer. She was the one who cataloged all the little repairs you just handled."

Ethan chuckled. "She's a one-woman historical society."

"She said it could be a jewel in the right hands." I paused. "I don't think she considers *mine* the right hands."

Chuckling, he wiped his brow. "She's just in love with history. If Dinah could press rewind on New Orleans, she would. I think it has to do with restoring her family's prominence in town. I heard that they used to rival the Means back before the War. But the Means family's star had risen while the Mercers' plummeted. She could be trying to bring back their former glory."

So Dinah's desire to preserve the town's history was personal. If she could control the narrative of the town's history, she could elevate her family's place in it. It was a useful fact to learn today, and it made me realize that Ethan was a resource just as good as Char and Sally.

"You've lived in New Orleans all your life. Would you say what's going on concerning Tabby Means is normal for your town?"

Ethan's expression said my question caught him off guard. It took him a moment to respond. "I'm not sure what you mean by *normal*."

"Murder, for example. It's not normal in New Orleans, I assume?"

"Not by any means." He ran his hand through his hair, considering. "It's not like it hasn't ever happened, but it's rare, and it's usually in the heat of passion."

"So something pre-meditated is even rarer?"

Ethan nodded. "To have someone plan something like what

supposedly went down with Tabby is not something I can remember ever happening."

"And what do you think about their suspect?" I was trying not to lead him but to find out his thoughts about Stanley without them being biased by my own impressions.

"Taz?" Ethan shook his head. "He's never struck me as the type, but I've heard rumors about his past. And you can't always tell who might snap and do something unexpected."

I figured that counted as a neutral vote, which was better than an automatic assumption of guilt, the rumblings of which I'd heard around town.

"There is one thing weird about the murder, though," he volunteered, standing close enough to my chair for me to make out his faintly woodsy scent. "I don't know why the murderer would try to make it look like a suicide. Anyone who knew Tabby also knew she was the type to lash out at others and not herself."

A bemused look came over his face. "One time, I'd been up at the Means' property doing some work for Vince. We were out by one of his sheds that was in the process of collapsing from rot when Tabby came charging across the lawn. She walked right up to Vince and slapped him across the face, then turned around and stormed off without saying a word. Vince just continued like nothing had happened."

My eyes widened. "Did you ever find out why Tabby slapped her husband?"

"I went into the house later to tell Vince I'd finished the job and overheard the two of them arguing. From what I could make out, they were fighting about evicting Tabby's mother from the land she's on. At first, I thought Vince was the one pushing for the eviction, but it really sounded like it was Tabby who wanted her gone. Which was confusing." He shook his head. "Maybe I got it all wrong. I don't know. Vince heard my footsteps and the argument stopped, so I can't be sure what all was said."

I watched as Ethan finished the lemonade, then nodded in some kind of southern gentleman salute. "Mind if I go wash up?"

"Help yourself."

Chonks started talking to him the minute he entered, and I heard the cat's little paws hitting the hardwood as he chased after Ethan before the door closed and muffled the sound. The silence gave me the opportunity to mull over what I'd found out from Ethan.

Why would someone have tried to make it look like a suicide? The obvious reason was to cover their tracks. If the sheriff and the coroner thought it was a suicide, they might not look closely at the body. But if suicide was so out of character, any local person would have known that the Rains siblings would see through the staging. Which meant the murderer was really trying to throw suspicion off himself and onto someone else.

Stanley had been arrested for the crime due to his being the last person seen with the deceased and his T-shirt being found at the scene. But if a young man the town called Taz was clever and careful enough to set up the suicide to cover his actions, why would he have left his shirt behind? It didn't make any sense. Unless someone had set it up to make it look like Stanley was the murderer.

But even that supposition had problems. Why move the body to the auto garage where one of Tabby's exes worked if the murderer was going to pin his crime on Taz? Nothing made sense with the clues as I understood them. I needed to talk to more people on my makeshift list of suspects.

Ethan came out of the house and was forced to persuade Chonks to stay inside. I couldn't help but smile at the exchange, even if it meant that the handsome handyman was about to depart.

"How much do I owe you?" I asked.

"The work was minimal, so let's just say it's on the house."

Another gift. The folks of New Orleans sure were generous. "I can't accept that. You did a lot of work today."

"Consider it a welcome gift. And when you need more substantial work, like these old houses often do, give me a call then."

"Thanks," I said, thinking that I could listen to his southern drawl all night long. Ethan was walking down the steps when I thought of one more use for his New Orleans-based knowledge. "Say, if one wanted to run into Vince Means, not by making an appointment or anything but just casually coming across him somewhere in town, where would be the best place to do so?"

The corner of the handyman's mouth quirked up. "Thinking about becoming the next Mrs. Means?" he asked, laughing.

I shook my head vigorously. "Oh, no! You have the wrong idea. I just—"

"It's okay," he said, his smile widening. "Vince isn't too social with most of us locals, but he's usually at the New Orleans Bazaar on Saturdays. He's a classic car aficionado, and his club usually meets in the municipal lot beside the bazaar. You might be able to accidentally encounter him there."

"I didn't mean…" I trailed off as Ethan walked away, waving over his head in a signal that said my protests didn't matter. I bit my lip, wondering if he was joking with me or if he actually thought I was the type of woman who would go after a man right after he'd buried his last wife, just because he had money.

"I bet this never happened to Miss Marple," I said, then opened the door to go inside. I'd forgotten the state Chonks had worked himself into, however, so the cat burst out of the house like a shot, and I spent the next half hour chasing him as he ran down the drive after Ethan's truck.

"I should just let you go!" I wheezed as Chonks did his best to evade capture. "You know they have gators down here!"

Chonks looked at me with a reckless air, as if to say gators had nothing on him. Maybe he was right. Any gator dumb enough to swallow that mass of fur was sure to have indigestion fit to kill it.

CHAPTER 9

The New Orleans Bazaar was meant to evoke the image of some crowded exotic marketplace with strange scents and unusual goods from foreign lands. The reality didn't quite match the name's aspirations.

A block of Main Street was lined with shade tents, under which folding tables displayed a number of wares. It was part farmers' market, part flea market, and part something unique to New Orleans. The number of people in attendance made me think that most of the town had turned out this weekend. I'd walked over from the library when my shift ended, and now I was scouting the parking lot for classic cars.

I managed to locate a group of cars that looked out of place. Their paint jobs were immaculate, their shapes sleek and expensive looking. I knew these were the classic cars Ethan had mentioned. There were a few men milling around outside them, but none looked like the description of Vince that Char had given me.

I had been hoping the doctor would be able to accompany me to the bazaar today. Having someone who could point out potential suspects in the throng would have been useful, but at the last minute, she had to beg off. "I've got a lead I'm running down. Hopefully, I'll be able to say conclusively how the drug in Tabby's system got into the killer's hands by this evening."

That piece of information was critical, so I'd encouraged her to pursue it, saying I could tackle the market alone. But I realized I was handicapped because I didn't know all the players in this little murderous melodrama by sight yet.

Fortunately, my lack of knowledge didn't turn out to be a handicap. Giving up on the cars, I figured it was worth at least scanning the bazaar to see if I could locate Vince or anyone else that was on our short list of persons of interest.

Tabby's mother and her mechanic ex-boyfriend were my additional targets, but based on what I'd heard of their reputations, I wasn't sure they were the type of customers the bazaar would attract. Still, the day wouldn't be wasted if I could at least get a feel for community sentiment. Would the residents of New Orleans be calling for Stanley's blood in retribution, or would I find others who thought him innocent of this heinous crime?

It turned out that my prime suspect was the most visible after all. I'd stopped by one of the booths that sold little felt toys stuffed with catnip, thinking Chonks might enjoy one. Then again, there was plenty of the real thing running around the old plantation house, so he might find the felt variety tame by comparison. Maybe his attraction to the mood-altering nip would make it preferable, though.

As one could tell, I took my stewardship of that fat furball very seriously.

A commotion arose at a nearby booth, and like most of the other folks around me, I turned to look for its source. The shade tent was a bright red, the tables underneath draped in crushed red velvet and lined with glass cases displaying homemade jewelry. A banner hanging from the tent canopy read "Merciful Adornments" in a loopy cursive script.

Mercy was behind the tables, her face flushed. "You can't do this!" she cried at a tall, well-dressed man outside the booth.

I realized from Char's description that the man she was addressing was Vince Means.

"I'm afraid I can," he said. "I can and I am."

I crept closer, noticing that several other members of the crowd were doing the same thing. All of us were pretending like we weren't trying to eavesdrop, continuing to browse the booths as we moved closer to Merciful Adornments. Except Dottie. Dottie didn't bother to pretend. She stood in front of the booth across from Mercy's, her mouth open in surprise, ignoring the ice cream cone in her left hand that was melting all over her antique lace gloves.

Hoping I was less conspicuous than Dottie, I picked up a crocheted shawl and pretended to examine it from a table two booths down from Mercy's. All the while, I snuck glances at the unfolding scene. The subject seemed to be Mercy's alimony payments.

"You must have paid off that judge to even accept a case like this!" The accusation rang across the bazaar, Mercy's anger filling the street with tension. Several bystanders stiffened at her tone.

Not Vince. He chuckled instead, shrugging one shoulder. "The case is legally valid."

"That's baloney! The alimony has been decided for almost a year. You can't just change it now on a whim."

"It's not a whim. New evidence has come to light."

Mercy scoffed. "What evidence? What could have changed? We're divorced."

"Evidence of infidelity." Vince reached into a case to pick up a piece of jewelry, but Mercy slapped his hand, making him drop it. He fixed her with an unimpressed look. "You were cheating on me during our marriage."

The dark-haired beauty's jaw dropped. "You have got to be kidding me. That's absurd!"

"The attorney doesn't think so. And soon, the judge won't either."

"You bastard," Mercy hissed. "You're the one who cheated, for chrissakes!"

"And every month, you make me pay for it." The hostility in his tone matched his former wife's. "If the judge sees things my way, you won't be able to bleed me dry anymore."

"Why are you doing this?" Mercy asked suddenly, and I could tell she was on the verge of tears. "I was a good wife to you. I even signed off on your farcical divorce papers. Why do you insist on continuing to torture me?"

"I could ask you the same question," he growled. "You want to make a fool of me, like all the other women around here. But that ends now."

Vince stalked off, and looky-loos scattering to get out of his way. Mercy yanked a tissue out of her purse and dabbed at her eyes, her breathing uneven. To have that conversation privately would have been upsetting enough, but to have it in front of half the town had to be as embarrassing as a dream of being nude in public. This might be a metaphorical exposure, but it was no less painful.

Unable to help myself, I put down the shawl and moved down to Mercy's booth. "Hey," I said softly, trying to infuse the single word with sympathetic feeling. "Are you doing okay?"

She laughed, but it wasn't a light sound. "Sure. I always enjoy a good public fight with my dreaded ex. Being threatened with poverty just adds spice to life, don't you think?"

Her sarcasm shamed me, and I apologized, about to give her space, but she shook her head. "No, I'm sorry. You don't deserve me lashing out at you. I'm just shaken up."

"I don't blame you," I said, giving her an empathetic smile. "If you ever want to talk about it, I'm around to listen." It would also give me the chance to learn more about Vince. And as much as it might have made me feel like a jerk, Mercy was still technically a suspect. The scorned woman could have taken her revenge on her rival.

Right now, Mercy didn't look like the type of person who could kill someone, even though she'd just gone head to head against her smarmy ex. Her face was puffy, her expression bereft. "I know you heard what was said," she said. "How could you not hear it?"

I nodded. Vince Means had a commanding voice, which often correlated with being a loud one.

She blew her nose. "He's trying to take away my alimony. It already amounts to little more than peanuts, and he wants it back."

"Isn't he like the richest man in town? That seems a little..." I couldn't think of a tactful way to say what I meant.

"Petty?" Mercy laughed again. "Spiteful? Yeah, that pretty much describes Vincent Means to a T." She took a deep breath. "He thinks I betrayed him, walking away when I found out about Tabby. I was just supposed to look the other way while he had his fling with that piece of human trash. But I have my pride too."

"How could anyone have expected you to stay after that?" I better understood her exchange with Tabby at the first book club meeting now.

Mercy sniffled. "When I first met Vince, he was so charming. Handsome, rich, funny. But after I became Mrs. Vince Means, I realized that he will always put himself first and that he expects complete loyalty, but he doesn't feel the need to return that loyalty. But even though he was running around with that young tramp, I never once cheated on Vince."

"He clearly thinks he can prove his case to the judge," I said. "Do you think he'd have any reason to believe you strayed?"

Mercy threw up her hands. "I don't know. Because he's a dumbass? I didn't cheat!" She caught her breath, her tone coming out more evenly. "I waited home at night, waited while he was out with that... female. Tabby Carter, the beauty queen. He met her when he was one of the judges of the *Miss Bon Temps* contest. Now we all know what she had to do to earn her crown. Or should I say, *who* she had to do?"

"She was sniffing around him nonstop. I saw it myself the night of the pageant. Tabby knew I was his wife, but that didn't stop her. She saw something she wanted and she wasn't going to stop until she had it. In that way, she and Vince were very well suited."

"No one could blame you for not liking Tabby," I said, my tone neutral.

She looked at me with a hard expression. "I didn't kill the little tramp. I despised her more than anything, but I'm not a murderer." She talked over my protests that I hadn't meant to offend. "My cousin is one of Sheriff Rains' deputies, and I heard from him you've been snooping around, trying to interfere in the investigation. So let me clear it all up for you. After the book club meeting, I went home and took a bubble bath to calm my nerves. And that's all."

"I'm not snooping. I'm trying to save an innocent man."

It was clear Mercy didn't give a hoot about my protests, though. She turned, looking past me, no longer interested in our conversation.

I debated purchasing a piece of jewelry to try and smooth things over, but I doubted it would work. Besides, to be honest, her creations weren't my style. The last thing I needed was a twenty-dollar necklace made of chunky plastic geometric shapes in garish clashing colors. I left the booth, following the path of Vince's steps and hoping to catch sight of him in the crowd.

I ended up back in the parking lot, but there were fewer classic cars parked there now. Vince was nowhere to be seen. It was probably a good thing, as catching him after his argument with Mercy could lead to another awkward conversation. Better to quit while I was ahead.

Today's trip to the market hadn't eliminated any of the potential suspects on my list, but it did give me some insight into Mercy and Vince's tumultuous marriage and its demise. Still, I was left with too many questions and not enough answers. I needed to talk to Vince, to get his side of the story.

Running into him didn't seem likely, so it was time for a direct assault. Tomorrow morning, I'd pay a visit to the refinery and see if I could get some face time with the boss.

CHAPTER 10

The St. Dismas Sugar Refinery sat on the outskirts of town, on land that had once been surrounded by sugar cane fields as far as the eye could see. The refinery was old. Its whitewashed surface had faded after years spent in what I was coming to call "the Louisiana hotbox."

I sat in my car as it idled in the parking lot, already dreading the sprint to the building's entrance. Cold air was blasting from the vents and I tried to lower my body temperature as much as possible while I gathered my thoughts. Before I had headed to the refinery, I'd stopped by the Tip Top to feed my pastry addiction. Sally told me she'd been to the jail the day before to check on Stanley and he didn't look good.

"He's losing weight," she'd lamented. "And I still can't get a word out of him. And if he's not talking to me, you can be darn sure he's not telling Sheriff Rains anything."

It was a reminder that an innocent life hung in the balance. The thought of a gentle spirit like Stanley being sent to prison for murder made my stomach threaten to eject its sugary contents. It didn't help that I'd learned Louisiana was a death penalty state.

The idea of waltzing into the richest guy in town's business and interrogating him about his dead wife wasn't in the least appealing, but I had to do it if I wanted to clear Stanley's name. If Vince was willing to rob his ex-wife of her alimony even though he had more money than half the town put together, was it really that far of a reach to think he might have been willing to get rid of his current wife if she wasn't behaving to his liking?

I turned the engine off, immediately missing the cool air. Climbing out of the driver's seat, I hurried toward the entrance, adjusting the blazer I'd worn because I thought it would make him take me seriously. Instead, it was already rumpling in the humidity, and I could feel twin wet spots growing under my arms.

Cursing my idiocy, I struggled to open the heavy door, tugging with all my might until the receptionist came out from behind her desk to pull it open. *Strike two,* I thought, falling for the classic "push not pull" blunder. At least the receptionist was cheerful.

Until I asked to speak to Vince Means.

She pursed her baby-doll-pink-coated lips and said she didn't have any appointments listed for Mr. Means this morning. I had expected a little resistance at getting in to see Means, so I'd prepared a tactic I hoped would work on Little Miss No.

"I'm sure Mr. Means is a very busy man, and I don't plan to take up much of his time, but I'm coming on behalf of," I leaned in conspiratorially and whispered, "the late Mrs. Means. She asked me to come here prior to—well, you know—and speak to her husband about the merits of a mobile library his employees could access. You know how important literacy was to the late Mrs. Means, of course."

The receptionist stared at me like I'd grown another head. "Uh huh."

"I'm doing this as a personal favor to her memory." Lowering my voice again and injecting it with a dash of stupidity, I went for the *coup de grace*. "We don't want her coming back to haunt us for not following her wishes, do we?"

The idea of a spectral Tabby lurking around the refinery seemed to do the trick. I saw her touch the little gold cross hanging from her neck.

"God forbid," she murmured with a little more force than was polite. She gestured toward the chairs lining the wall. "Give me a minute. I'll see if Mr. Means is available to see you."

Sitting down, I let out a huge breath. Although I'd displayed as much confidence as I could muster, I hadn't really expected to pull this off. Telling myself not to start counting hatching eggs in one basket yet, I tapped my foot against the floor nervously, going over the script I'd rehearsed all last night in my head.

The receptionist returned more quickly than expected, so I fixed her with an eager smile. From the look on her face, I thought Means might have told her to give me the brush off, so I was surprised when she said Mr. Means would see me now.

I followed her down a hallway lined with windows. At the end, an imposing walnut door stood closed. The receptionist knocked twice, then turned the knob, opening the door and motioning me through.

I entered the office, taking it in as I made my way toward the seating area in front of the wide wooden desk. The ceilings were high, exposed girders crisscrossing above them. The walls were a mixture of stained wood and exposed brick. Two large windows sat behind Means, backlighting him like he was the subject of a work by one of the Dutch masters. I swallowed, even more nervous than before.

"My receptionist said you were sent here by Tabby?" he asked as I was sitting in one of the plush chairs in front of him.

I nodded, a little taken aback, expecting to exchange some pleasantries first.

"Correct," I said, crossing my legs carefully and putting my folded hands primly in my lap. "I had mentioned my idea of a mobile library to her after our book club meeting, and she encouraged me to come see you." I launched into my cover story, gaining confidence as I went. "As you likely know, the hours of the library overlap with the hours of the employees on your biggest shift. Since they can't get to the library, I figured we could bring the library to them."

I went through a few statistics I'd memorized about how reading improves cognitive performance and how I could include professional development selections to build a better workforce. For his part, Vince Means looked bored.

"I could bring by my offerings once or twice a week. I could even organize a book club over the lunch hour if there is enough interest." As he glanced at his watch for the second time, I started to lose steam. Figuring it was time to get to the real reason I was here, I weaved Tabby back into my story. "We could call it the Tabitha Means Memorial Library Extension, in honor of your lovely wife. And let me offer you my condolences. She's in a better place now."

Vince let out a huff of air, something halfway between a scoff and a laugh. "That all?"

I nodded, even though I hadn't found the opening I'd been hoping for. Still, I wouldn't give up. I wouldn't let Stanley go down just because I was scared off by some bulldog businessman. "You know, Tabby mentioned to me that she was joining the book club at your behest. She'd even admitted that she wasn't fond of reading herself."

Vince just stared at me, saying nothing. Desperate for a way past his iron demeanor, I took a risk.

"She's very different from your first wife, if I may say so. Mercy is also a book club member. It seems the community is very passionate about literacy, which is why a mobile library is such a good—"

I'd apparently struck gold because Vince interrupted. "That's enough of that. No one wants you bringing around a box of moldy books once a week. I know Tabby wouldn't have sent you here with an idiotic idea like that. I have my doubts that she could even write her own name, let alone understand a work of literature. I sent her to that dang club because I wanted her out of my hair for one night a week."

My eyes widened but I tried to keep my expression blank while he unloaded on me.

"I'm not interested in your mobile library idea, just like I'm not interested in filling you in on gossip about either of my wives. Now thank you for stopping by, but you can go ahead and get out now." Vince stood, gesturing toward the door.

I took the hint and stood to go. "Thank you for your time," I said softly as he led me to the exit.

As he passed, I noticed his collar had a smudge of lipstick on the inside. It was the same baby pink his receptionist was wearing.

Outside, it was even hotter than when I'd entered. I was beginning to think that my uncle had sent me to New Orleans as a punishment. He'd enticed me with the world's most perfect home library, only to torture me every time I had to leave said library.

I raced to my car but paused when I noticed that a lunch truck was pulling up alongside a few picnic tables in what must comprise the refinery's break area.

It wouldn't hurt to grab something before I headed to the library to start my shift. The pastries I'd had for breakfast were long digested, and I didn't want to be dependent on the lone vending machine next to the library's bathrooms. I approached the truck, digging my wallet out of my purse while eyeing the menu.

Stepping up to the window, I was surprised to notice the older woman inside it was wearing a black armband over her kitchen whites. Glancing around the confines of the truck, I noticed an old photo stuck to the far wall with peeling tape. Although I hadn't known her for long, I was able to recognize Tabby Means in the photo.

"What can I get you?" the woman asked, and I recognized that she shared some similarities with the girl in the photo. Their features were similar, but this woman was clearly older, with sun-bleached skin and dirty-blonde hair in a style that was at least twenty years old. Could this be Tabby's mother?

"Turkey sandwich and a lemonade."

"Be right up."

I'd managed to beat the lunch rush, it seemed, because I was all alone at the truck. This was my chance to continue the investigation, and I couldn't waste it. "You have my condolences. I didn't know Tabby well, but she seemed like a fine young lady."

The woman glanced up at me, her eyes evaluating me before they returned to her work. "*Fine young lady* ain't how people generally describe my daughter. So yeah, I'd say you didn't know her well."

It wasn't the response I was expecting, but I knew from Char already to expect a curveball from Tabby's mother.

"I'm sorry. This must be a tough time for everyone." I wasn't sure what to say that wouldn't seem intrusive.

"Everyone but the man inside that building who killed her."

I started. "Beg pardon?"

Tammy looked at me again. "That damn Vince Means. He didn't even give my girl a proper funeral, just a graveside ceremony during her burial and with no one but family allowed. What kind of a sendoff is that?"

I figured that Char had it right. Tammy was upset at her missed opportunity. It seemed rude to think that way about a woman who'd just lost a child, but she didn't seem like a woman who was afraid to express herself.

"Didn't even get a wake," she said. "Not that any of the stuck-up people in this town would come to any wake I throw, even though I was her mother. Too busy keeping their self-righteous noses up in the air."

Tammy passed the sandwich over and filled up a cup to the brim with ice before dumping in some lemonade from a plastic picture. "Here."

She turned away, paying me no further attention.

"You think Vince killed your daughter?" I asked, trying to sound scandalized.

Tammy turned around, attracted by the call to drama. "I *know* that sorry bastard killed her. Tabby told me she had something on him, something that could ruin him in this town. Two weeks later, she shows up dead. You tell me. Doesn't that sound like proof positive?"

"Did you take this to Sheriff Rains?"

Tammy turned her face to the side and spit on the floor, her face covered in a scowl. "We ain't the type to go to the law to handle our business for us. That sheriff hassles us so much as it is that I wouldn't ask him to whiz on me if I was on fire."

"Sorry for your loss," I mumbled, taken aback by her response, and I started in the direction of my car.

A whistle blew, making me jump, and workers in coveralls started spilling out of the building. I carried my sandwich and drink into my car, rolling down the windows instead of starting the car. I'd have to speed to make it to the library on time, but I didn't want to miss the opportunity to watch Tammy Carter for a few moments.

I didn't consider Tammy a suspect. She was Tabby's mother, after all. But her hatred of Vince was clear, even though Vince had stood up for her against her own daughter when Tabby wanted to evict her—if Ethan was to be believed.

I unwrapped the sandwich, took a bite, and chewed slowly while I watched the workers order their own lunches from the truck.

I finished my sandwich by the time the crowd started to thin. Looking up from my lemonade, I saw Tammy exiting the food truck and lighting a cigarette. She waved at one of the coverall-wearing employees, a tall man with a mop of curly hair. He walked over to her, bending down so she could kiss him. Tammy looped her arm through his and they headed over to the bank of ashtrays by the picnic tables.

I realized that spying on Tammy wasn't getting me anywhere but late for work. Glancing at my phone, I saw my shift at the library started in less than fifteen minutes. The thought of facing Luanne's wrath had me racing out of the parking lot, hoping Sheriff Rains didn't have any of his men stationed on the highway that led into town.

CHAPTER 11

The dream had started simply enough. I'd been riding in an old roadster, the wind whipping through my hair. Looking down, I realized I was wearing a loose velvet dress, old-fashioned and not at all like my normal wardrobe.

I looked to the driver's seat and saw a well-dressed man there. His profile was familiar, although his clothing was like mine. Antiquated, like something out of the Roaring Twenties.

Glancing back to the window, I watched as ashen fields blurred at our sides. "Look at them go past," I murmured.

"Past," the driver said, drawing my attention back. "Can't repeat the past? Why, of course, you can!"

His look was half-crazed, but when I heard his voice, I realized who he was. It was Stanley. The moment I grasped this fact, his clothing shifted. It was still old timey, except for the Tasmanian Devil T-shirt.

His voice filled with determination. "I'm going to fix everything just the way it was before. She'll see."

I had no idea what "she" he was referring to, but suddenly, the car jerked from an impact. I screamed and tumbled over…

And landed on the floor next to my bed. "Holy moly," I muttered.

Chonks lifted his head to look over the edge of the bed at me. Seeing I was in no real danger, he blinked twice and went back to sleep.

I checked the clock. Since it was practically dawn, I didn't bother trying to return to bed. Besides, I didn't want to risk falling right back into the dream. It had been jarring, seeing Stanley there. Guilt hit me, guilt at failing to uncover the truth about Tabby's murder.

The dream stayed with me throughout the day, my anxiety increasing. By the time my shift at the library ended, I'd decided to go over to the jail to make sure Stanley was okay with my own eyes. When I arrived, however, Sheriff Rains was not so eager to see me.

"He's fine," he barked when I asked to check on Stanley. "Miss Sally's in here just about every day, bringing him some treat or another."

"But does he eat them?" I fired back. "Or does it end up in a uniformed belly instead?"

He narrowed his eyes, his hands on his hips. "We don't take kindly to accusations without proof."

"Funny you should say that because that's basically what you're doing to poor Stanley! There are plenty of other good suspects. Like the ex-boyfriend, for instance. Or her not-so-loving husband."

His eyebrows shot up. "I see someone else doesn't know how to mind their business. I told Char on Saturday that if I caught her snooping around again, I'd make sure she lost the coroner gig." He looked me up and down. "I might not be able to fire you from the library, but I can cite you for interfering with an active investigation."

"Why Stanley though? Why not Jimmy Beal or Vince Means?"

"Because they both have alibis that check out," he replied. "So unless you know something I don't, the prime suspect is still Taz Lane."

"Tabby's mother thinks Vince killed her because Tabby knew something about him that would be disastrous to his business. He might have an alibi, but that doesn't mean he couldn't have paid someone to bump her off."

The sheriff ran a hand through his hair and let out a sigh. "You got any evidence to back that up? Or just the word of a substance-abusing petty criminal?"

I could see this was getting me nowhere. "I don't have evidence yet, but—"

"There is no *yet,* Miss Hastings. You're gonna stop sticking your nose where it doesn't belong."

"I'm not stopping until I figure out who did this and you let Stanley go!"

Rains seemed to sense I was bordering on a display of emotion, and like most alpha-male types, he did what he could to prevent it.

"I'll take you back," he said. "You can visit with him but not for long."

I followed the sheriff out of the office area and down a long brick hallway that led to an area with two identical cells. One was empty, but in the other one, I could see Stanley, his eyes trained on the floor, shoulders slumped.

I approached the cell, but Rains stopped me, pointing at a white line painted on the floor. "Stay behind it."

"Hi, Stanley," I said softly, waving at him and then feeling foolish for doing so. My greeting got no response, and I was struck by how forlorn he looked in his oversized jail jumpsuit.

"I'm here to help you. Several of us know you couldn't have done what you're being accused of. We're trying to figure out who did, but if you know anything that can help us help you, you need to tell me."

"It was nice of you to come all the way down here just to do my job for me," Rains said behind me.

I turned around. "Have you been able to get him to talk?" I asked, my tone confrontational. "Been having long intimate conversations? Or better yet, did you get a confession out of him?"

Rains' eyes narrowed and I wondered momentarily if I'd pushed things too far. I held up my hands and took a deep breath. "I'm sorry. What is it going to hurt to let me have a try? You're right here, so you'll hear everything, and if he says that he did it, then I'll actually be helping you out."

The sheriff swept his hand out in front of him as if to say *be my guest, crazy lady*. I turned back to Stanley. He wasn't going to respond to my questions about that night, not with the tension high enough to choke us all. No, I needed to try to connect on another level. We'd bonded over books. Maybe that would work to draw him out now.

"The book club hasn't been the same without you," I told him. "I'm not even sure most of the women are reading the book." I let out a laugh, hoping for at least a smile from Stanley, but he sat there, still.

"I thought maybe you and I could talk about *Gatsby* since we're both fans. I keep coming back to something you said during our first meeting, that everyone in the book traffics in lies, either the lies they tell others or themselves. I've been wondering about those lies. Do you think a person knows they're lying, or do you think they could believe a lie so well that it becomes the truth, after a fashion?"

Stanley finally looked up at me, a lost expression on his face. I was about to apologize for blabbering at him when he finally spoke. "Lies beget more lies. They don't become the truth. Subjective belief is a powerful thing, but it doesn't change objective reality."

The world had underestimated Stanley Lane, and every time he opened his mouth, I was even more impressed by his intelligence. "Even Nick's lies are transparent, and as the narrator, he paints the reality of the story. He detested Gatsby by his own admission, from beginning to end, and yet he tells him he's better than the bunch of rich idiots who attend Gatsby's parties."

"A rotten crowd," I murmured.

Stanley nodded, his eyes brightening. "Tabby was part of that crowd," he said suddenly. "Like the girls in that book, the ones who come to Gatsby's house to drink his liquor and flirt with men who aren't their husbands."

"What happened that night?" I asked softly.

"She asked me to come to her house, to help her find a few things in the house's library since she was convinced I knew a lot about books and she didn't want to look like an idiot in front of her husband."

Stanley looked into the distance, and I wondered if he was remembering that night. "I believed her, believed that she wanted to impress her husband and that she was afraid that he found her inferior. In a way, she was like Gatsby, having elevated herself to chase the one she wanted but never realizing that wealthy people like Vince Means will always see through her because she isn't like him and she never will be."

He was the first person to humanize Tabby, and it made me suddenly sad for the girl that most folks considered a nuisance at best and a curse at worst. "Did you go back to her house with her?"

Stanley nodded. "It was dark when we got there, which Tabby didn't take well. She mumbled something about evening the score that I didn't entirely catch. We went to the library and Tabby offered me a drink. I refused, so she poured herself one and drained most of it in one long swallow. Then she refilled her glass.

"I tried to get her to focus on what she'd brought me there for. Instead, she 'accidentally' spilled her drink down the front of my T-shirt, then insisted I take it off so she could wash it for me. But once she pulled it over my head, Tabby laughed and shoved the shirt down her skirt so I couldn't grab it back from her."

His cheeks were flushed, and his voice started to stumble. "She started touching my… my chest. She even kissed me. I don't like to be touched, and… and I didn't want… she's a married woman. So I told her I was sorry I couldn't help her, and I ran out of the house and walked the two miles home."

Stanley wouldn't meet my eyes, ashamed of having fled.

"It's not your fault," I reassured him. "Did anyone see you walking home?"

Shrugging, he finally met my gaze. "It was dark, and I don't remember seeing any cars."

"Is this the first time anything like this has happened with Tabby?"

His gaze flicked to Sheriff Rains, then back to the floor. "Yes." The way he responded made doubt blossom in my stomach, and I wondered what Char had said about Tabby in high school.

"Is there anything else you can remember?" I asked, hoping against hope there was something we were missing. "Anything that might have seemed out of place?"

Stanley shook his head. "Not that night, but there was something. Something that happened when I was delivering groceries a few months back. When I got to the Means house, Tabby answered the door and had me carry the groceries into the kitchen and put them away."

I goggled at that. Making the delivery boy put your groceries in your fridge and cabinets? That was a new level of imperiousness.

"I did what she asked, but while I was working, I heard a noise in the hallway and went to look. That's when I saw Tabby kissing someone. Someone who was not Vince Means."

My eyes widened. "How do you know it wasn't Vince?"

"He was wearing coveralls and a baseball cap," Stanley replied. "Vince Means doesn't even wear coveralls to work on his classic cars, so I knew it wasn't him."

"Any idea who it was then?" Rains drawled.

I turned around to give him a dirty look for interrupting. He ignored me, focusing on his prisoner.

"No. His back was to me, and like I said, he was wearing a ball cap."

"So Tabby was having an affair with someone else, and she came on to you?" I asked. "I think we can establish that she's an unfaithful spouse, which means Vince would have even more motive to have her whacked."

"Okay, that's enough," Rains said, gently gripping my arm to pull me back from the cell as I strayed closer. "Time to go, Junior Detective."

"I'm going to figure this out, Stanley," I called back as the sheriff led me down the hall. I frowned when I saw his head was bowed, his mouth muttering words I mostly failed to catch. Something about green lights and false hopes.

"You've had your fun, but now it's time to go home," Rains said when we were back in the office.

"I don't know how you can be so cavalier about this. You just learned that Tabby was having an affair. And that T-shirt? It was clearly planted at the scene by the real killer."

The corners of his mouth turned down sharply. "Nothing Taz just said clears him of the crime, and no one can back up his story."

"What about the lipstick I saw on Vince's collar when I stopped by his office? It matches the color his secretary was wearing."

"You went to Vince's office?" When I nodded, the sheriff let out a sound of annoyance. "You're not to approach anyone with your speculations anymore, do you understand? Stop trying to sabotage this case."

"Do you get paid extra to act so stubborn? I'm trying to solve the case!" My frustration with the St. Dismas Parish Sheriff Department knew no bounds.

"You're going to stop snooping around before you end up getting hurt. Not everyone appreciates you poking around in their business."

"Is that a threat?"

"It's a warning. Stay clear of this case, and let the professionals do what they're trained to do."

"It's very reassuring to know our tax dollars go to arresting the wrong man. Maybe next, we can hand out tickets to people who don't speed or who park within the lines." I stalked toward the door, my temper close to boiling over.

"Or we could use them to send nosey northern folk back where they came from," he called after me.

CHAPTER 12

The roommate's new friend sneezed a lot.

I knew that some humans were weak, their systems unable to handle the awesomeness that was the feline species, but Char wouldn't surrender to that weakness. She bravely attempted head pets even though her eyes were puffy and her nose leaked like a faucet.

"I'm sorry about Charlie," Char was saying as the roommate poured her another glass of wine. "He's a good guy, but he's got a blind spot when it comes to his job. As sheriff, it doesn't look good if someone is going around checking up on his work. Doesn't exactly inspire confidence, you know? And I know how he feels. It's like the way everyone threatens me with Dr. Loomis's second opinion. The old man is on his way to blind, for goodness sake!"

Jade didn't seem ready to forgive Char's brother, and I made a mental note to make him feel my claws at my first opportunity. "Well, your brother isn't blind, but he might as well be. He knows that Tabby was cheating, and he knows about the lipstick stain, which means it's likely Vince was cheating too."

"Not to play devil's advocate," Char said, opening a box of crackers and digging inside it, "but lots of people cheat on their spouses and no one ends up dead. Unless we find something that can connect the affair to the crime, we've got nothing."

"What about what Tammy said? That her daughter had something on Vince that would ruin his standing in town? That could be motive for murder, right?"

"Sure, it could be," Char said, snatching a cheese slice and stacking it on her cracker. "It could also just be an angry woman acting out and flinging accusations any which way."

Jade slumped against the table, putting her head down and letting out a frustrated groan. That made it the perfect time for me to jump up on said table and display my behind as close to her face as possible.

"Chonks!" she complained, picking me up and settling me in her lap. "Behave yourself."

I allowed her to stroke my back for the moment, wondering what they planned to do next in their novice-style investigation.

"Did you find out anything about the drugs?" Jade asked hopefully.

"Nope." Char frowned. "And my brother found out I was snooping around and told me he'd find a new coroner if I couldn't let him do his job."

"Oh yeah. Your brother did say he'd fire you." Jade bent down to shove her face into the ruff of fur at my neck. "What do we do now, Chonks?"

Meowing never did any good but I tried it now. All it did was provoke a half-smile on my roommate's face. Then she bent over and set me on the floor. I set off, bored with their conversation.

Besides, I already knew who the murderer was.

I'd figured it out the night the book club descended on our new digs. I could smell it then, just like I could smell it the first night I'd gone out the broken basement window in the middle of the night and snuck into town. I'd been staring at the decorations in the window of a storefront when I'd caught sight of movement inside. I'd smelled something on the figure who'd come out. Something faint. Something damning.

Now that I thought about it, those windows reminded me of

something Jade had been reading me just the other day. I didn't know why it was taking my roommate so long to catch on. Silly human.

I knew who killed Tabby Means, and I knew how they did it. But because humans were dependent on their dumb mouth sounds for communication, I wasn't able to tell Jade what happened. I'd been dropping clues for her to find, but so far, she hadn't caught on.

It would be so much easier if my roommate were a cat. Then again, I supposed one of us had to make a living to keep us in kibble.

I debated curling up in the streak of sunlight on the sitting-room floor, but what I was really craving was a session with the handyman with the magic fingers. Ethan Millbank gave the best pets of any human alive. I wanted him back here quick.

But if I had to leave everything to my roommate, she'd never get up the gumption to invite him over. The last time Jade had let a man know she was interested, I was barely weened. That meant it was up to me to get Ethan back.

And I had just the thing.

These old houses had a lot of things that went bump in the night, not all of them supernatural. I'd already scoped out something the humans had hidden from themselves and I believed I'd found a way to get the roommate to call back the handyman for a full investigation.

Soon, I would just have to roll over on the rug and expose my belly to those magic fingers. Sure, I would still bite, but I'd let him get in a good massage beforehand.

But first, there was something I had to do. Returning to the sitting room where the girls were making their way through the bottle at a healthy clip, I pulled a stealth move, creeping behind the couch, then circling the room so that I could approach unseen.

Like a mythical warrior cloaked in shadow, I suddenly sprang, revealing myself as I leapt on Char's lap and immediately put my paws on her chest.

"Chonks!" she said through clogged nostrils. "You want a hug?"

I rubbed my head against the side of her neck, setting off a flurry of back-to-back sneezes that made Char let out a string of curses afterward. But by then, I was already running down the hallway, set on my act of sabotage.

I was a cat who knew what he wanted. And right now, I wanted someone to scratch behind my ears with fingers that felt like they'd been made for feline worship.

Ethan Millbanks, come back to me.

And Jade too, I suppose.

But mostly me.

CHAPTER 13

I sat bolt upright in bed, letting out a little shout as sleep abandoned me in favor of confused fear. "What's going on?" I asked, the words slurred with grogginess.

A sound comprised of a metallic screech and a softer rhythmic tapping rang out again, and I realized that it was this disturbance that had awakened me. I didn't know where the noise was coming from, but it was the third time tonight it had jarred me awake. I grabbed my phone to check the time and frowned, figuring that getting up early might just be my new thing.

I was making coffee and debating the source of the sound when the doorbell went off. It was still early, especially for house calls, but since I was up already, I might as well see who it is. Whoever it was, I hoped they were prepared for the sight of me in my fluffy pink bathrobe and slippers.

Carrying the cup of coffee to the front door with me, I was surprised to find Dinah Mercer on my porch. She greeted me with a bright smile that reminded me of a televangelist's wife. "Hey there!" she said, her chipper voice making me wonder if she was one of those ungodly morning people.

"Hey," I said, my tone more subdued. "What brings you over here so early in the morning?"

Dinah looked past me and into the hallway, as if trying to gauge whether an antique chandelier could be installed in the entryway. "I noticed on my way up the steps that the loose board is fixed. I applaud you for making repairs to this beautiful home." She ran her fingers across the doorframe with the awe of a teenage girl petting a horse for the first time.

"As you said, I can't afford a lawsuit."

Dinah ignored my acerbic tone and launched into the pitch that would have dragged me out of bed if I hadn't already been woken up by the noise. "I wanted to see about adding your house to the historical homes tour of the area." She pulled out a pamphlet and passed it to me.

It was a glossy color brochure containing a map of St. Dismas Parish with stars representing the antebellum mansions in the area, and wide-outs from each star had a picture of the home. There were six homes listed. Dinah wanted me to be lucky number seven.

"Did you ever talk to my uncle about this opportunity?" I asked, trying to hand the brochure back.

"Keep it," she said, refusing to receive it. "And yes, but he always insisted on maintaining his privacy, and as it was clear he wasn't well, I respected his wishes. But you?" She looked me over and shrugged a shoulder. "You're young and healthy and just the sort of owner we'd love to have on the tour."

"I'm sorry—" I began, but she cut me off, waving her hands in front of her.

"Hear me out. I'm hoping to open a historical museum in New Orleans in the next few years, and it could bring more tourists to our little hamlet. Tourists mean more money in our coffers, which could translate to more money for the public library, for instance. So everyone wins."

"Dinah, I think that idea has merit, but—"

"I'm so glad you think so!" She pulled out a neatly typed piece of paper and handed it to me. "Here's a list of improvements that would not only recover some of the glory of this old house, but it would make you stand out from the other houses on the tour."

I stopped reading after the list suggested I repaint in the "historically appropriate" colors of mint and ebony. "I can't afford all this on my salary."

"Well, dear, you could always sell." Dinah looked around as if sizing things up. "I myself would offer a fair price for the property. In fact, you might not know this, but one of my cousins built this house himself, back when it had been surrounded by fields of sugar cane. If you sold it to me, I would promise to lovingly restore it to be a testament to both our relations that have gone home to Jesus."

My eyes widened at her last remark. "I'm sorry, Dinah, but I don't think it would be right to sell this house. My uncle wanted me to have it, and he passed it on to me for a reason." I didn't let her know that I had yet to figure out what that reason was. "I appreciate the offer, but—"

"This is just too much house for one person," she interrupted, changing tactics. "I don't know how you're going to keep up with it. I can show you a nice little property in town, one that won't cost a fortune to maintain. Not to mention, it will save you a bundle on your tax bill. I'm sure your uncle doesn't want you knee deep in property taxes."

"Uncle Mike left a trust to pay property taxes and help with upkeep. I'm sorry, but I'm quite happy here and I don't plan to sell."

"I see," Dinah said, her excitement fading. "Well, if you change your mind, here's my card."

I took it, then bid her goodbye and watched her walk to her car. As she drove away, I went back inside, returning to the kitchen to freshen up my coffee. I tossed Dinah's card on the table, but I hung the map of the parish up on my refrigerator, figuring it might come in handy. The list of suggestions went into the recycling.

When I turned around, I noticed Chonks on the table, pawing at the card. Suddenly, he snatched it up in his mouth and jumped off the table, running off down the hall.

"Crazy cat," I said, shaking my head. Chonks was always running off with some thing or another. He'd somehow gotten one of Mercy's earrings the night of the book club meeting and I'd only found it later when he was carrying it around in his mouth.

Taking a long drink of coffee, I felt the last of the cobwebs leaving my brain. Dinah Mercer was an interesting woman. Polite but pushy, she seemed to live more in the past than in the present, always trying to bring things back to the way they were. The problem was, while the past might be rosy to some, to others, it was nothing worth revisiting.

"I got news for you, Dinah," I muttered to myself as I made my way to the shower. "The old times weren't so great for everyone." Sure, some folks had mansions but others weren't so lucky. Like in *Gatsby*. The fashionable high society houses weren't that far from the valley of ashes, after all.

I was in the shower when I heard the clang again, loud enough this time to make me jump and almost slip. After my shower, I dried off, got dressed, and tidied up before it was time to head into work. Like every other morning, I had the exciting task of scooping out Chonks's litter box. It was my least favorite thing about cat ownership, and if I could have taught him to scoop it himself, I would have.

I hadn't even gotten to the first scoop when I noticed something sticking out of the litter. Grabbing a paper towel, I used it to pick up the item, which turned out to be Dinah's card.

"Chonks!" I yelled. "What has gotten into you?"

Finishing up with the litter box, I was walking down the hall when the mysterious sound rang out again. From this location, it sounded not so much like a clang as a long, mournful moan. My skin broke out into goose pimples, and the notion that the source might be supernatural scrabbled across the surface of my mind.

"No," I said to myself as I started walking again. "Jade, you will not start thinking this place is haunted."

Chonks looked up at me from his place at the end of the hall, his expression giving me the feeling he was chiding me for being ridiculous. "I know, buddy," I told him. "No ghosts and ghouls here. Just something in need of repair, right?"

The cat looked at me a moment longer and ran down the hall to the entrance to the kitchen, where he stopped and looked back, his tail swishing. I followed him into the kitchen, and he took off again, running to where the old-fashioned phone hung on the wall. Chonks batted at the long, curly cord a couple times, and I laughed.

"Okay, okay. But you know that phone isn't connected, dummy." Still, I got the message he was trying to convey, or the message I was attributing to him at least. I doubted his cat brain was smart enough to know he was even standing under a phone.

Pulling out my smartphone, I tapped Ethan's contact. Expecting to get his voicemail as I had the last time, I was caught off guard when his deep voice answered with a husky "Good morning."

The reason why I'd called him eluded me at the sound of his amazing drawl.

"Uh, hi there," I said. "How's it going?"

His chuckle made me feel warm all over. "It's going. Just calling me for a chat, or did you need something?"

I really wasn't prepared to go into what I needed because the images in my head right then were decidedly not appropriate, but I did recall the original reason I'd called. "Actually, I was wondering if you might be free sometime this week to stop by and check something out for me."

"Sure. What do you need me to check out?"

Oh, the things I wanted to say in reply to that questions. "Er, well, I'm not exactly positive."

I could hear his confusion over the line even though he said nothing for a few moments. Then came a drawn out, "Okayyyyyy."

"Sorry, I know I'm not making much sense. Long story short, there's a noise in my house that sounds like the banshee's southern cousin. Although I'm a fan of haunting gothic tales, I doubt there's a spectral entity roaming the halls of my house."

Ethan laughed. "Sounds like maybe your furnace is having a conniption."

"Maybe so. When can you stop by?"

"Let me check my schedule and I'll text you and let you know."

"Thank you."

His voice dropped an octave, making my toes curl. "Jade, if it is the banshee's cousin, make sure you read the Bible backwards to stave off its evil cry. Best to use a southern accent, though, so the banshee's cousin can understand you."

It was my turn to chuckle. "I thought it was *Gone with the Wind* I was supposed to read backwards. Good thing you warned me."

I hung up, a smile on my face, and not just because of the silly southern superstition joke.

I felt Chonks swishing through my legs and looked down at him. "Okay, furball. Your new best friend will be over later this week."

Chonks purred loudly in approval.

CHAPTER 14

The trailer looked like it was held together entirely by rust. A few random items dotted the yard, a tractor tire, some cinderblocks, and a birdbath full of brown water. In the driveway sat the food truck, silent and empty.

"Are you sure this is a good idea?"

Char shook her head. "No. But how else are we going to figure out what Tabby was holding over Vince's head? It's not like Vince is going to tell us."

Another run-in with Tammy Carter wasn't something I was looking forward to. There was something off about the woman, besides her penchant for the dramatic. Women like Tabby weren't born into a vacuum. I had a feeling Tammy might not have been the perfect mother.

Before we could get out of the car, the front door of the trailer opened and Tammy walked out, her arms laden with a box that was overflowing with hamburger buns. She tossed it to the ground next to the food truck and opened the truck's side door with a big jerking motion.

We got out of the car and walked across the lawn. I was mindful for any hidden dangers that could be lurking in the crab grass as we crossed.

Tammy turned around, a suspicious look on her face. "Can I help you girls with something?"

I waved as Char put on a bright smile. "Hi, Miss Carter. We came to pay our respects. Your daughter was a part of our book club."

Tammy's expression went from suspicious to disbelieving. "Book club? Tabby ain't the type to join any kind of club, especially one for books."

Char went charging past that fact, trying to pull Tammy past her doubt. "It's a shame about the funeral being private and all. Her book club friends weren't able to say our last goodbyes."

"Take that up with Vince Means," Tammy barked.

"How did Vince behave at the funeral?" I asked. "Did you notice anything out of the ordinary?"

Tammy looked me up and down. "You were at the refinery the other day, weren't you?"

I nodded. "You said you thought Vince was responsible for what happened to your daughter."

Nodding, Tammy slammed the door shut on the food truck. "That man's slicker than a river snake. He ain't afraid to do what it takes to get his way, even if it ain't exactly legal."

"Do you have proof?" Char asked, causing Tammy to let out a burst of angry laughter.

"Proof? Come on, girl. You know he's too smart for that. Vince covers his tracks."

I frowned. "Does Vince know you think he killed your daughter?"

"Vince don't give a damn what I think. Neither did Tabby, for that matter. It's probably the only thing those two agreed on."

"It seems strange that they would get married if they didn't get along." This was from Char, who tried to inject genuine confusion into her voice, but I wasn't sure if Tammy would buy it.

Tammy pulled out a pack of cigarettes from her pocket and lit one up. Taking a long draw, she blew out a cloud of contemplative smoke. "Anyone could see what Tabby wanted out of the marriage. Money.

Clout. Respect." Another long inhale, another smoky exhale. "Vince? Well, his hormones was leading him around by the... you know."

"Still doesn't mean he had to marry Tabby," Char replied. "As much as Jesus might not approve, plenty of men take up with younger women."

"Don't I know it," Tammy said with more force than expected. She eyed us both. "Y'all were her friends, huh?"

Char and I nodded in unison, and Tammy pursed her lips. "Tabby ain't got many friends, mostly because she stabbed them all in the back, or the front, a few too many times. But maybe it was different with y'all."

She leaned in, looking around conspiratorially. I felt suddenly like I was in a stage play, and we were in front of some great invisible audience. The feeling was so strong that I even looked around to make sure we were still standing in an overgrown yard filled with debris.

"Most of the town knew Vince and Tabby were running around together. Hell, Tabby made sure of it. She wanted to be the next Mrs. Means, and she wasn't afraid to do what it takes to get that title. That's another thing she had in common with Vince."

"What did she have to do?" I asked, almost breathless in anticipation. Tammy knew how to turn a mundane conversation into melodrama, and I was falling under her spell.

"Only the same thing women have been doing for ages." Tammy took her hand and moved it in the shape of a semi-circle over her midsection.

"Tabby got pregnant?" Char asked, surprise evident in her tone. "But they never had a baby."

Tammy winked. "She told Vince she was pregnant. What happened to that baby? I don't know. My money is on it never existing. In any event, it worked. Vince managed a quickie divorce and then Tabby got her white wedding."

I realized my mouth was standing open and shut it. The thought that people would lie about something so massive was astounding. No wonder Mercy hated Tabby with a passion. "But even if Tabby was...

in the family way… that didn't mean Vince necessarily had to marry her."

Tammy laughed hard enough to set off a coughing fit. "Girl, you know you're livin' in the Bible Belt. That means whatever sin goes on below the belt has to be paid for. Folks in town would have blacklisted Vince for not doing right by my daughter. And Tabby would have raised such a stink, it would have been impossible for Vince to sweep it under the rug."

"You think Vince could have found out about the fake pregnancy and that's why he wanted to be rid of Tabby?" Char asked.

Tammy dropped her cigarette and stepped on the butt to put it out. "I'm sure he had his suspicions, but I don't think Vince would have bothered. Tabby got what she wanted, so she wasn't a threat. And one wife is as good as the next with that sort."

The implication was that his eye would continue to wander, regardless of who wore the Means wedding ring around her finger. In that regard, Tammy was a very good judge of character, if the lipstick on Vince's collar was any indication.

"You said that your daughter had something on Vince, something that would turn the town's sentiment against him. Do you have any idea what it is?"

Tammy inhaled and let out a huff of air through her nostrils. "She wouldn't tell me. That girl and me have had our own issues. But whatever it was, it was big. Big enough for Vince to try and screw me over as well."

"What do you mean?" I was so engrossed in her tale that the only thing I was lacking was a box of buttery popcorn.

"This," she said, jerking open the food truck door again and leaning inside to dig in a storage container on the floor. She pulled out a piece of crumpled paper and thrust it in my direction.

Taking hold of it, I tried to straighten it out to get a good look at it. The logo at the top was a stylized M, the script below it announcing the "Means Co." It was an eviction notice with Tammy's name on it.

"He wanted me out by the end of the month. Makes sense that he would wanna get rid of me if he was planning to take my baby out. Didn't matter that we had a deal. He was still gonna throw me over."

"A deal?" Char asked.

Tammy nodded, opening her mouth to speak, then froze. This was the first time she'd hesitated since we started our conversation. "Yeah, a deal for this property. It was tied to the food truck here. I agreed to park it at his place exclusively during the lunch hour, and in exchange, he discounted my rent."

I didn't know Tammy well, but I knew she was holding something back. She grabbed the notice back, tossed it in the truck, and slammed the door once again. "Anything else you girls need? I gotta get dinner in before my man gets home from work."

"This is an awkward question," Char said, "so forgive me if you think it's rude, but do you think Tabby could have been seeing anyone else?"

Tammy chuckled, pursing her lips. "Honey, I'm sure she was. That girl was always runnin' around with boys. She started chasing Vince when her and Jimmy were still together. And I even seen her flirt with my man. That stunt got her put out of my house."

"Any idea who she might have been seeing?" I asked, amazed at the sort of dynamic Tabby and her mother must have had.

"Take your pick from any of the eligible guys in town. Even the ineligible ones." She looked at her phone and frowned. "Now, if you'll excuse me, I gotta get going."

"Thank you for your time," I said, then felt like an idiot for saying it. Char and I returned to the car while Tammy hustled into the house and shut the door behind her.

"Well, that was a whole lotta nothing," Char said as she fastened her seatbelt.

"You think so?" I asked.

She nodded. "It's all speculation or hearsay, no hard proof."

"What about the eviction notice? It does line up with what Ethan overheard."

"But there's no way to say how it's relevant. And I didn't buy whatever 'deal' she said she had with Vince. Why would he discount her rent to have her park her food truck at the refinery? Where else does she think she could make any money with that rolling culinary monstrosity? If anything, I could see Vince charging her extra to park there."

I frowned, forced to agree with Char. Talking to Tammy had just raised more questions than answers. The only thing we knew for certain was that Tabby wasn't afraid to lie to get her way, and she had a fondness for gentlemanly company.

I put the car into gear and headed back toward downtown. "What do you think Tabby could have had on Vince? What would be bad enough for him to kill her over?"

Char shrugged. "Your guess is as good as mine. If a fake pregnancy and a string of affairs wasn't enough to make Vince balk, I don't know what would be enough to make him risk his business and his life to murder his wife."

"He could have paid someone to keep himself out of danger. Hired someone to do his dirty work."

"Then he'd have another person who had a secret on him. It doesn't seem worth it." Char scratched her head. "You know, the idea of dirty work brings me back to something you said Taz mentioned. The man in coveralls at Tabby's house, the one she was kissing. Jimmy wears coveralls at the garage."

"It's as good a lead as any. She was found dead at his place of employment." I'd called the garage the day after they arrested Taz to make an appointment, but it seemed like I wasn't the only one whose car suddenly needed maintenance. They'd been so swamped that I'd had to wait over a week to get an appointment. Tomorrow was my timeslot.

"It looks like you're going to get your shot to interrogate Jimmy 'The Hunk' Beal." Char chuckled.

"The Hunk? Is he good looking?"

Char nodded. "If you like a guy with tattoos and dirt under his fingernails, he's not too bad. But that's not the only reason they call him that. He was known as 'The Hunk' because he could fix any 'hunk of junk' around, according to his bragging. Although my brother used to say they called him that because his brain worked about as well as a hunk of metal."

"I thought moving to a small town was going to make my life simpler," I said.

Char laughed. "Well, look on the bright side. The word 'simple' definitely describes Jimmy."

CHAPTER 15

The exterior of American Auto Garage was painted red, white, and blue, no doubt in homage to our nation's colors. Why it was patriotic to get your automobile serviced, I had no idea, but the little slice of Americana that was the auto garage was neatly kept and very clean. It seemed the owner ran a tight ship.

I got a glimpse of said owner when I walked through the front doors and stepped up to the service desk.

"You got an appointment?" the bald man behind the counter asked. He was a wall of muscle with piercing blue eyes. A jagged scar ran from his right cheek to a spot behind his chin. In his mid-fifties, he had an unmistakable air of sternness.

"Yes, uh, Jeff," I said, reading the name patch on his pristine coveralls.

"Folks around here call me Scar, which means you ain't from around here." He eyed me. "If you just came down here to get your crime scene jollies, you can take yourself elsewhere."

I swallowed hard. "I need an oil change. And I am from around here now, technically. I live in the big house off Beechum Road."

Scar grunted. "Pull your car into bay two. If I find out your oil don't need changing, I'll refuse you service the next time you come in."

I hurried outside and hopped into my car, piloting it into the garage bay as commanded. It was clear that Scar did not play around, and frankly, I was already terrified of the big man.

A tall, attractive young man in tight blue coveralls guided me in with hand signals so that the car would be correctly positioned on the lift. Climbing out of my car, I confirmed his name was Jimmy, per his name patch, as he looked down at a clipboard, his longish blond hair falling in waves around his striking face. "Oil change, right?"

"Yep. Although I always get my oil changes promptly as the manufacturer suggests, so the oil might not seem very dirty..." I trailed off, hoping what I said was enough to prevent the owner from sanctioning me.

He gave me a crooked smile that lit up his face, and I decided "The Hunk" wasn't a misnomer, at least in terms of his physical attractiveness. I also noticed the knuckles on his right hand were tattooed in an intricate vine pattern. I could also see the hint of another tattoo creeping up his neck, the bulk of which was hidden by the coveralls.

"Most folks wait in the waiting room," he said, pointing out the glass-walled reception area where a line of plastic folding chairs stood in front of a console television so old, it might have been the first one ever built.

"I think I'll stay out here if you don't mind. The guy in there is just a little intimidating." *And Mardi Gras is just a little parade.*

Chuckling, Jimmy waved his hand as if waving away my worries. "He comes off as hard, but he's got a good heart. Was a sergeant in the Iraq War, and they used to ask him how come he never sweat out there in the desert. He said he was born in Louisiana so he wouldn't sweat even if they stationed him on the Devil's ball sac."

I blinked at the colorful turn of phrase, and Jimmy shook his head and apologized for his rude talk. He started to gather supplies, getting ready to change my car's oil. "It's okay," I said. "I'm from Baltimore so I've heard it all."

He nodded. "Yeah, I've seen you around town but haven't had the chance to make your acquaintance yet. I'm Jimmy." He held up his right hand, covered in dirt from working on cars all afternoon. "Forgive me for not shaking."

"My name's Jade, and I'm the new assistant librarian."

"Ah, that's where you've been hiding out. I don't make it in there very often." His expression said he had never seen the inside of the library in his lifetime.

I laughed, then looked around. There were cars in the other two bays, and I could see through the glass partition that Scar was on the phone, likely taking down another appointment. "You guys have been busy lately, eh?"

"Yep," Jimmy said, nodding.

"Do you think it has anything to do with the murder?" I figured directness would work best on The Hunk.

Jimmy looked up, a little surprised. His expression turned thoughtful. "Yeah. I reckon it does."

"I heard you were close with Tabby. I'm sorry for your loss."

He shook his head. "That was a long time ago. I ain't been with Tabby for ages." I watched as he clambered under the car to start draining the oil. He unscrewed the oil filter, his hands getting coated in oil in the process.

"Any idea why someone would plant her body here?" I asked while he traded out the old filter for a new one.

"None in the slightest." His tone was a little tight, but I wasn't willing to let the issue go. This could be my only chance of talking to Jimmy, so I had to make the most of it.

"A lot of rumors have been flying around town, and I've heard your name tossed around a time or two."

Jimmy let out a grunt as he replaced the filter. Then he wiped his hands on a shop rag and gave me an angry look. "That's ridiculous. Just because someone dumped Tabby here doesn't mean I had anything to do with it. Besides, the cops already arrested that mentally challenged kid from the grocery store."

I restrained myself from defending Stanley. "Some folks don't think he could do it. They think it must have been someone closer to her, someone with whom she had a history."

"I know what the people around here say. That I was running around with her behind Vince's back. It's not true. Once she got with Vince, I wouldn't touch her."

"Is it true she left you for him?" I tried to ask the question in a neutral tone, but it still felt intrusive. I wasn't used to performing an interrogation.

"Yes," he said, scowling. "Tabby was a wild child. I should've known she was cheating on me. But I loved her, as dumb as that was, and it came as a shock when she dumped me for that old fart." He held up his hand, showing off the tattoos I had noticed earlier. "These used to be her name. Had them covered up on the same night she married Vince."

I believed him. Sincerity rang from his voice. But that didn't mean he couldn't still have killed her. People kill the things they love all the time.

"Love isn't like a switch, something you can turn on and off. Are you sure you didn't have any lingering feelings for her?"

"Sure. Maybe. I don't know." He threw down the rag and let out a breath. "Maybe for a while, but I wasn't seeing her again. Once bitten is twice shy for me."

"And yet her body still showed up in this garage."

"I got an alibi, and I already told the sheriff about it. I was over Tabby, and I'm seeing someone new. So whatever evil thoughts you have in your head, lady, it wasn't me!"

I nodded, wondering who The Hunk was making time with now. Before I could ask, he let out a string of curses. "People been in and out of the garage all week, asking me these same hateful questions. I didn't kill my ex-girlfriend!"

I held up my hands and lowered my voice, hoping to calm him down. "I understand, and I'm sorry if I upset you, but if you aren't the one responsible, Tabby's body being found here is even more suspicious. It's almost like someone was trying to set you up. Is there anyone who would want to pin a heinous crime on you?"

His laugh was cynical. "How should I know? I didn't think I had any enemies, but the way everyone is treating me now, I can't tell who to trust."

"I'm sorry," I said, meaning it. Putting my hand on his arm, I backed off on the interrogation. "This must be very difficult."

"You have no idea."

I was about to ask him about his alibi, but I didn't get a chance. Scar charged out of the service office, his voice booming across the garage. "It's just a dang oil change. You should be done by now."

"Yes, Drill Sergeant," Jimmy said, his voice weary.

"Watch it with the disrespect, boy. If I was your sergeant, you'd be cleaning the latrines with a toothbrush. Finish up and get on the Chevy that was supposed to be ready yesterday."

"I can't help it that every busybody in town wants to crowd in here and get a look at the crime scene!" Jimmy's frustration was palpable.

Scar, however, wasn't affected by his employee's complaint. "If you'd been here working late on the Chevy that night like you were supposed to be, then you wouldn't have had to worry about your ex being found dead in my garage."

"Something came up," Jimmy said.

"Yeah. Another skirt to chase." Looking down at me, Scar jerked his head in the direction he'd just come. "Let's go inside and settle up, ma'am. You can flirt with him on his own time."

"I wasn't flirting with him," I said, but Scar was already walking away, expecting me to follow. I looked back at Jimmy, but he was focusing on the car. I hurried after the sergeant, not wanting to make him any angrier than he already was.

Back at the service desk, I watched as Scar wrote up the paperwork by hand. The phone rang, but he ignored it this time.

"Pretty busy around here," I said, just to fill the awkward silence between him.

Scar grunted. "You're not the first single female who gets all tingly flirting with the handsome murder suspect."

"Oh, I wasn't. I wasn't flirting. I'm actually trying to help my friend, Stanley Lane. He's been wrongly accused of this crime and I—"

"You work for the Sheriff's Department?"

I blinked. "Uh, no."

"The District Attorney's office then?"

"No. I'm a librarian."

His stone-faced expression didn't need a verbal accompaniment. He handed me the paperwork and showed me where to initial. I handed him my credit card, feeling like all kinds of moron.

"Still, Stanley is my friend, and if I can find out anything that could help him out, I'm going to try." Screwing up all my courage, I decided to go for it. "Do you—uh, that is—what are your thoughts on—"

He looked at me and ran my card. "I don't have an opinion. That girl was fast and loose. And Jimmy out there ain't a white-knight type. He didn't like the fact that she was going behind his back with Vince. Almost cost me a fortune when Vince brought in his Porsche and dummy out there screwed up the wiring, probably on purpose."

He handed me back the card and sighed. "Still, Jimmy is more vacuous than vicious, and I don't think he could have had anything to do with Tabby's demise."

"You think he was over her?"

"I think he started seeing someone new. Jimmy ain't the type you can keep down for long. Short attention span. He forgets to stay mad at you."

I couldn't help it. I laughed. "Any idea who this mystery woman is?"

Scar shook his head. "No clue."

The door to the service office opened and Jimmy walked in, handing me my keys. "I pulled her around front for you."

"Thank you," I said. "Please tell your boss that my oil was dirty enough to come back again."

Jimmy's puzzled expression was adorable, and I managed to get a laugh from Scar, so I counted myself as ahead for the day.

As I steered in the direction of home, I went over what I'd learned. Jimmy seemed like a straight shooter, or at least he was good at playing dumb, because I didn't see him as someone able to pull off the kind of logistics Tabby's murder and crime-scene staging would have required. Still, there were a couple of red flags that made it so I couldn't eliminate him from my list.

For one, Scar said he'd screwed up the wiring on Vince's Porsche. While it could have been an accident, Scar hadn't seemed to think so. Fooling around with a car's wiring sounded dangerous. Maybe he had been banking on it causing a malfunction that could lead to a crash or worse.

And the mystery woman. Apparently, she was Jimmy's alibi. But who was she? The way gossip burned through New Orleans like wildfire, I would have expected it to be common knowledge by now. The fact that it wasn't meant he was hiding something.

I had to find out who the mystery woman was. Or if she even existed.

CHAPTER 16

"You're following too close! He's going to see us."

I frowned. "You could have driven!" I was trying to stay two car-lengths behind, but New Orleans was small, and the lack of traffic wasn't cooperating.

"He knows my car better," she said. "Besides, I needed my hands free to give these donuts the attention they deserve."

I let out a snicker. Char was obsessed with her snacks. I didn't know how she stayed so trim. Good genes, I supposed.

"He's turning," she said, her energetic expression making powdered sugar fly off her lips. "Don't miss the turn!"

"I won't!" I couldn't help myself. I dissolved into giggles.

We'd decided that the best way to figure out the identity of the mystery woman was to run surveillance on Jimmy. Our plan was to tail Jimmy when he left the garage and see where he went. Which was why we were currently following behind him, my co-pilot yelling out random directions while she plowed through the donuts we'd brought along for the ride.

Before long, we discovered Jimmy was headed home. Home just happened to be the same trailer park where Tammy lived.

"Must have been convenient for the lovebirds in high school," Char commented.

I parked down the street so as to not raise suspicions, and we sat tight for an old-fashioned stakeout. In less than an hour, the bulk of the donuts had disappeared. By hour two, we were bored enough to play I Spy. We'd just passed the three-hour mark when there was a commotion from the backseat.

Chonks leapt suddenly into the front seat, scaring the bejesus out of us both.

"Where the heck did you come from?" I hugged him to me and lifted him so I could see his expression. "You're supposed to be at home. What part of 'indoor cat' do you not understand?"

The cat let out a lazy mewl, unimpressed by my questioning. I set him down, and he immediately lashed his tail right under Char's nose, making her sneeze. Char reached for her purse, digging inside to locate her allergy medicine. As she popped a pill into her mouth, Chonks jumped on her lap, knocking the bottle to the floor.

The crazy cat leapt after the bottle, batting it around on the floor of the car.

"I'm sorry," I said, trying to grab it from him as he kicked it over to my side of the floorboard. "He's an unrepentant rascal who refuses to behave like a gentleman, no matter what I do."

I managed to pry the bottle away from Chonks, who'd grabbed it and hugged it to his chest like a linebacker with a football. Holding it up, I realized the prescription had been filled at Mercer's pharmacy.

Nothing surprising about that. The entire town probably gets its prescriptions from Mercer.

I passed the bottle back to Char, who returned it to her purse, much to Chonks's displeasure. He let out an angry yowl, and I told him he had to behave himself if he was going to join our stakeout.

My bladder had just given me the signal that it wouldn't be tolerating the situation for much longer when a car finally approached Jimmy's trailer. Its lights were off, which was suspicious enough, and it pulled up to a stop just long enough for a passenger to jump out and rush up the steps to the trailer.

"I don't know whose car that is," Char remarked. Then she noted a rideshare logo in the back window. The trailer door opened and the figure ducked in, the door shutting tight afterward.

"Could you tell who it was?" I asked Char, but she shook her head, and I admitted that I couldn't either. "What do we do now?"

"Well, we know they're in there. We could sneak up and peek in the windows, see if we can see who's in there that way."

My eyes widened. Following someone in my car was one thing, but creeping up to the windows and looking inside seemed like going too far. "Are you serious?"

Char nodded. "This is desperate measures time. We have zero evidence, and it won't be long until the trial gets moving. And since I doubt Taz is going to testify, the trial isn't going to last very long. If we're going to get him out of jail, we're going to have to take a risk."

I closed my eyes, gathering my courage. "Okay. We find out who it is, and then we go."

"Right." Char opened her door and climbed out.

I turned around to where Chonks had climbed into the spot beneath the rear window. "You stay put and be quiet."

Chonks gave me the look of a child claiming innocence while standing in a pile of opened presents on Christmas morning. I shook my head and got out of the car. My heart was pounding, my palms clammy. I shoved my hands into my pockets and jogged after Char, who was already approaching the trailer.

It was a rectangle with windows on the far end that were covered in cheap white blinds. Although they were lowered, the edges of the plastic had turned up on one of them, enough to get a look inside.

Pressing my face to the window, I peered into what turned out to be a bedroom, and not a particularly tidy one. Clothes were cast around the floor on thick brown carpet that could disguise a multitude of sins. An unmade bed, a nightstand littered with candy wrappers and half-empty sports drink bottles, and a poster of a nearly naked female on a sunny beach completed the picture.

I shook my head at Char and we moved around to the back of the trailer. The first window we came on was narrow and frosted, likely the bathroom. Moving down to the next window, I narrowly avoided tripping over the remains of some kind of car exhaust system.

Char had ducked under the window, waiting for me to catch up. Dingy curtains hung to either side, the center part bare. Char held up her fingers, counting down 3-2-1, and we both crept upward to steal a simultaneous glance inside.

It was the kitchen. Like the bedroom, it was less than pristine. We only risked a quick glance before ducking again, but as neither of us had seen anyone, I risked a longer look. There was a sink full of dishes, a small table piled with mail, and counters piled with paper bags, empty cups, and the other debris of a bachelor pad.

Char put her hand on my arm, grabbing my attention. She jerked her thumb at the next window that was a few feet down. I nodded and followed her, giving a wide berth to the jumble of lawn implements left leaning against the side of the trailer.

This window had a set of gauzy white curtains that were fading to a dull yellow after years of sun bleaching. They were pulled across the entire window, but they were transparent enough to see through them for the most part. Char did her countdown and we slowly crept from under the window to peer inside.

The view this time was of the living room, and directly across from the window we stood before was the couch. Two figures were sitting there, and I reflexively ducked, holding my chest because I thought my heart was going to leap out of it.

Char rolled her eyes at me, then motioned for me to look again. Creeping upward a second time, I stayed long enough to realize who was sitting on the couch next to Jimmy.

"That's Mercy Means," I hissed in Char's ear. "Vince's ex-wife."

"I know," she whispered back. "What is she doing here? Could they be plotting together?"

"Maybe. I'm going to get a better look." I took a couple of steps to the left, trying to see past a fold in the fabric. Unfortunately, I'd forgotten about the pile of lawn tools.

My foot hit half the tines on a rake, making it shoot forward and disturb the other equipment piled there. With a loud racket, they tumbled against the trailer before hitting the ground. A dog two trailers down started barking like crazy, adding to the chaos.

I stood there, eyes wide, hands clapped over my mouth, a look of shock on my face that would be comical if the situation wasn't so critical. Char slapped her hand against her forehead and grabbed my hand. "Come on. We gotta run."

We dashed back toward the street, but before we could reach the end of the trailer, Jimmy came around the corner, a pair of nunchucks in his right hand.

"Hey!" he shouted. Then his jaw dropped.

"Dr. Rains? Is that you?" His eyes flashed to me. "And you were in the shop yesterday."

"Hi," I said lamely.

The neighbor's outside light flashed on, and Jimmy scowled. "Y'all better come inside before you get the whole park going."

I felt like a recalcitrant child, walking with my head down as I followed Jimmy into the trailer. Mercy let out a gasp when she saw us, jumping to her feet. "What are they doing here?"

"I was just about to find that out," Jimmy said.

I shrugged, trying to pretend it was no big deal. "We learned you were seeing someone new. A mystery woman. We followed you home and waited to see if we could find out who that mystery woman was."

Jimmy shook his head as if my explanation wasn't sinking in, but Mercy scowled. "You *followed* him?! What business is it of yours who he dates?"

"We're just trying to help Taz," Char replied. "He didn't kill Tabby. We're trying to figure out who did."

"I thought your brother was the sheriff," Mercy retorted. She turned to me. "And I thought you got enough at the bazaar. You still think I killed Tabby?"

Jimmy turned to her. "You, babe? This chick came into my garage asking me if I killed Tabby." He turned to me. "How could you think Mercy did it? That's screwed up."

I raised my hands to calm things down. "We're just trying to figure out what happened that night. Tying up loose ends."

"She couldn't have murdered Tabby, and neither could I," Jimmy said. "We spent that night together. Met up at a hotel over in Laplace after your little book club." He glanced at Char. "And I already told your brother the sheriff the same thing. Mercy gave him the damn hotel receipt. He had the decency to say he'd be discreet. Looks like I can't trust you two to do the same."

Mercy fell back against the couch, her hand over her face. "I knew it was just a matter of time before word got out that we were together."

"Why are you guys even bothering to sneak around?" I asked. "You're both single. Why not just date openly?"

"For one, there's the age difference," Mercy said, brushing her bangs off her face. "It might not matter if a man Vince's age dates a girl Tabby's age, but me dating Jimmy isn't going to be judged by the same standard. Not here in New Orleans."

"Who cares what people say?" Char said. "They'll get over it eventually."

"It's not that easy," Mercy said. "Vince is trying to take my alimony away, saying I was already seeing Jimmy before we were divorced. It's a lie, but I did start seeing Jimmy not long after the divorce was final. And the way Vince is, I wouldn't put it past him to manufacture evidence showing I was having an affair. Or heck, just find a judge he could pay off."

Char frowned. "Why would a guy like Vince want to take away your alimony? Is it a hefty sum we're talking about?"

Mercy let out a bitter laugh. "Barely enough to cover my monthly bills, and I live much more modestly than I did when I was wearing his ring."

"Vince is a spiteful snake," Jimmy hissed. "That's reason enough."

"I need that alimony," Mercy moaned. "It isn't much, but until I get my online sales increase, I need that money to get by."

"I'm sorry, Mercy," I said, linking my arm through Char's and pulling her toward the door. "And Jimmy, my apologies as well. I know that snooping around and invading your privacy is a rude thing to do. Please believe that we would never do it if it wasn't absolutely necessary."

I said a rushed goodbye and led Char out the door. We hustled toward the car.

"Wasn't that exciting?" Char asked and giggled like a little girl.

I looked at her like she might be modeling a straitjacket. "You've got to be kidding me."

"I only have one thing to say," she said, giving me a smile. "First one to the car gets the last donut!"

She took off like a shot, leaving me in her dust.

CHAPTER 17

Chonks was curled up on the front dashboard, keeping an eye on things. He let out an inquisitive mewl when we opened the doors and climbed inside. Char pulled up the donut box, opening it to reveal a solitary donut with pink icing and sprinkles.

She'd beaten me back to the car, but now she held up the donut, a look of masked disappointment on her face. "We can split it if you want," she offered.

"I'm good," I said, and the smile that hit her face was elated. "I don't know how you can think about food right now. Not after what just went down."

"I don't know how you can think about anything other than food," she said between bites. "Donuts are delicious."

Chonks let out a yowl that said he agreed and started sniffing at the contents of Char's hand.

"Get out of here, you porker," I said, picking him up and tossing him gently into the backseat. "Just sit still until I can get you home."

I started the car and put it in gear, rolling slowly toward the park exit. I was just about to ask Char if we should call the hotels in Laplace, just to confirm Jimmy and Mercy's story, but before I could speak, there was the sound of a slamming truck door.

We were coming up on Tammy's trailer, and that was where the commotion was taking place.

"You get back inside this house," I heard Tammy holler, the tone of her voice tinged with alcohol.

Whomever she was yelling at wasn't in the mood to follow her orders because the engine fired up and the truck began backing down the driveway at a breakneck pace.

"Don't you dare leave!" Tammy howled as it went.

I slammed on the brakes to make sure the truck didn't swing wide and accidentally hit us. As it backed up, I noticed the person driving the truck was the same man I'd seen her with at the refinery. The truck made it onto the road and took off like a shot, the tires squealing as it sped away into the night.

"Looks like her hot date didn't go according to plan," Char said.

I watched as Tammy stood there, looking off into the distance in the direction the truck had gone. She pulled out a cigarette, puffed it for a moment, the turned around and went back into the trailer, the screen door slamming behind her.

As I headed out of the trailer park, I wondered what kind of life Tabby had led. Her formative years were spent in this place, with a mother who didn't seem to like her very much, at least not as much as she liked the bottle. It wasn't hard to see how Tabby would crave an exit from this kind of life. Vince Means must have looked like a first-class ticket to paradise in comparison.

We returned to my house. Stepping out of the car, I was hit by the heat of the night that remained unbroken. A chorus of frogs sang around us, and Chonks started getting antsy in my arms. "Behave, buddy, or I'll put bars on all the windows."

He looked at me like I was the ridiculous one. We climbed the steps up to the covered porch where fat moths slowly circled the porchlight. I handed the keys to Char so she could unlock the door while I made sure Chonks didn't bolt.

I tossed him inside and shut the door behind us, then leaned back against it and let out a long breath. "I'm not sure if I'm cut out for all this snooping and sneaking."

Char patted me on the arm and smiled. "Oh, come on. You did great."

I pursed my lips and looked at her in annoyance. Char tried to disguise her laugh as a sneeze, but I still knew it was a laugh. "You have to admit it worked."

I shook my head. "It worked to tick them off."

"I don't think Mercy or Jimmy had anything to do with Tabby's death. Nor do I think they were conspiring together."

"They could have met in Laplace after the murder..." I trailed off, not even believing my own supposition.

"My brother would have found out what time they arrived and when they left the hotel. He might be a jerk, but he's a decent cop."

"I suppose you're right. But if it isn't Mercy or Jimmy, that brings us back to Vince and the possibility that he hired someone to get rid of his wife for him."

Char frowned. "Where does someone go to hire a contract killer?"

I shrugged. "Beats me." We wandered into the kitchen, and I pulled a bottle of fruit wine out of the cupboard. "Night cap?"

"Yes please." Char went over to the refrigerator where the map of St. Dismas Parish hung. "What's this?"

"Compliments of Dinah Mercer," I replied. "She wants to buy my house."

Char let out a laugh. "Sounds about right."

I handed her a glass, and I gently tapped my wine glass against hers. "To snooping on your neighbors and friends."

"To St. Dismas Parish," Char countered.

We both took a long drink, and I let out a sigh of refreshment.

"Your house isn't on here," Char said, pointing at the spot where my house should be on the map.

"Not yet. All I have to do is join the tour of homes, after investing a substantial sum to restore it to its past glory. Or I can sell it to her. Her cousin built this house, you know."

Snickering, Char shook her head. "By her telling, the Mercers built half the mansions in Louisiana." She pointed at one of the stars on the map. "This is her family's estate, the one she's been funneling her real estate commissions into for decades. And that's the old cabin her ancestors supposedly built when they first arrived in the parish." She gave me a sheepish grin. "I only know that because she's given me a lecture on her family's arrival in Louisiana not less than three times. I've started faking medical emergencies to get out of conversations with her."

I leaned in for a better look and noticed that the home wasn't far from the location of the St. Dismas Sugar Refinery. "That's awfully close to the Means land."

Char nodded. "Dinah is always pestering people to sell their historical properties to her. A couple years ago, she approached Vince about partnering on a restoration project that would bring in 'unlimited tourist dollars,' if you hear her tell it. She wanted to put a museum on their joint land as a tourist attraction."

My brow furrowed. "She mentioned opening a museum a couple years from now. Vince must have agreed."

"On the contrary, he told her to go build her museum up her own skinny behind."

My jaw dropped. "Are you serious?"

"Oh yeah. I heard it myself. It was right after the Papa Noel Christmas Parade last year. The Mayor had several prominent businesspeople on stage with him while he gave his annual Christmas address. Local business owners sponsor the parade every year. But while Travis was giving his speech, Vince and Dinah had a heated exchange, and it ended with Vince's—shall we say—strong 'no.' He said it loud enough for all of us to hear even without a microphone.

Shaking my head, I wondered what I'd gotten myself into moving to this town. "If Vince turned her down, then why did she tell me she's opening the museum?"

"Maybe she found another location," Char said. "Who knows? But once Dinah sets her mind on something, she doesn't let it go."

"Stubbornness seems to be a common trait around here. Maybe someone should test the drinking water."

Char doubled over with laughter, almost spilling her glass. She straightened, then held up her glass in salute. "The smart ones stick to wine."

A sudden ghoulish shriek pierced the night and I jumped. Char let out a whoop and crouched. "What the heck was that?"

"I wish I could tell you. My guess is either the heating system has gone wonky, or there's a ghost trapped in the walls."

"Sure, every good plantation house has to have a ghost. For yours, my guess is the ghost of Tabby Means. She's going to haunt you until you discover the real murderer."

"I'm sure. But I did put in a call to Ethan, just as backup. Maybe he can fix whatever's going on—or perform an exorcism."

Char gave me a teasing smile. "I guess any excuse is a good one to invite over a cute handyman."

The next day, that same cute handyman was knocking on my door. Chonks stood beside it, yowling in impatience while I opened the door. Inviting him in, I apologized for my cat's enthusiasm.

"You miss me, buddy?" Ethan asked as he crouched to scratch the eager cat behind his ears.

Chonks let out the loudest purr I'd ever heard. Once they'd had their heartfelt reunion, I informed him of the trouble I'd been having.

"It's a loud noise, like a screech at times, and at others, there's like a faint rhythmic tapping."

"Do you know where it's coming from? What area of the house?"

I frowned. "Not really. It sounds like it's coming from somewhere in the walls, but it echoes through the house."

Ethan nodded. "I'll listen for it. In the meantime, I'll have a look at the furnace."

I showed him the entrance to the basement. Ethan went down the stairs and Chonks followed, his tail waving like a happy little flag. I shook my head and retreated to the library.

About twenty minutes later, Ethan poked his head in. "The furnace looks fine, and I haven't heard the noise yet."

"It mostly happens late at night, if you really want to hear it." As soon as the words escaped my lips, I realized how they sounded. "Not that I'm, uh, inviting you to spend the night or anything. I'm just..." I trailed off, my cheeks bright red.

Ethan chuckled and suggested I follow the sound to its source if possible next time. If I could locate where it was coming from, he could come back and fix it.

"Yes, I'll do that," I said, embarrassment burning in my belly.

Chonks let out a plaintive meow and stood on his back legs to bat at the tools on Ethan's belt. "There's my assistant," he said with a laugh. "Trying to borrow some of my tools?"

Chonks sprang up, somehow managing to grab the end of Ethan's tape measure. He was off like a shot, down the hall, causing the tape measure to unspool as he ran with it.

I expected it to hit its limit and shoot backward, re-spooling itself, but instead, Chonks's velocity managed to yank the entire tape measure off Ethan's belt. It was clattering down the hallway as the cat skittered around the corner and out of sight.

"I'm sorry," I said, my face turning an even brighter shade of red.

"It's fine. I have others. My assistant clearly has a project he needs to borrow it for."

I walked Ethan out, apologizing for the lack of noise. "I won't call you out again until I've figured out where the ghost is hiding."

"Ghost?" he asked with a chuckle.

"Yes. Char said all good plantation houses have them. I've just got to figure out where mine has concealed itself."

"I'll let Father Knox know that he'll be hearing from you soon. He handles the supernatural. I'm just a handyman."

I watched him walk down the steps and head to his car. Ethan was so easygoing, and he never held it against me when I made a fool of myself. Making a fool of myself seemed to be a common event nowadays.

I'd peeked in windows, followed people home, interrogated them at their jobs. I'd badgered the sheriff, pried into a mourning mother's private business, and pumped honest people for information at every opportunity. Not once had I come away looking graceful or clever.

No, I was certain that by the end of this, New Orleans would consider me a fool.

"It doesn't matter," I said to myself as I closed the door behind me. "As long as Stanley is exonerated." That was what was important.

Refocused, I returned to the kitchen to grab a glass of lemonade before going to hide out in the library in the air conditioning for the rest of the day. At the fridge, I noticed Dinah's map again and pulled it down. I took it back to the library with me to study.

There was something bothering me about the historical society museum, something I couldn't quite put my finger on. The map didn't produce any insights, so I decided to do a little digging into the town's history.

Sometimes working in a library had its perks.

CHAPTER 18

The library was quiet that morning, like most mornings. A few older patrons were going through the periodicals, whether out of interest or just to enjoy the coolness, I wasn't sure. Luanne had claimed the circulation desk once again, confirming my suspicions that she didn't care for re-shelving.

I didn't mind today because re-shelving also gave me a chance to read up on the history of St. Dismas Parish. It was perfect cover, searching for the books I needed while I re-shelved others. It turned out there were only a few resources that talked about the local history in any detail. One in particular seemed to have the information I was looking for, so on my break I pored over it, making quick notes.

It seemed that the Means family had been in St. Dismas Parish since it was created in the first decade of the nineteenth century. Letters at the time referred to the land where New Orleans would spring up in later years as "The Means' Expanse."

Other plantations were mentioned soon after, so either the Means started parceling their land out or the "Expanse" hadn't entirely belonged to the Means. The Mercer name appeared a couple decades after the founding of St. Dismas Parish, but it quickly became clear that they were a major player in the area as well, as Ethan had suggested previously.

I looked into the sugar refinery next. The refinery itself was modernized, but some of the outbuildings had been around since the early 1800s. The Means family mansion was considered one of the finest examples of antebellum architecture in the state.

If Dinah craved control of the town's narrative, then having the cooperation of the Means family was a must. Either her joint collaboration was to include the land around the refinery, or there was another property Vince owned that Dinah wanted in on.

I put the history book down, then ran my fingers through my hair. I needed more information, stuff that I wasn't going to find in the library. Glancing toward the windows, I could see City Hall sitting across the street. They would have property records, survey maps, even registers that could give me an idea of what was once Means and once Mercer.

I knew I was on a wild goose chase since I couldn't articulate what, if anything, this had to do with Tabby's murder. But if Vince was the only suspect left and his alibi was air tight, he would have had to convince someone else to do the deed. Someone he could trust not to let the crime come to light.

Money might get him a long way toward his goal, but a paid mercenary could be tempted to talk, if caught, to avoid the death penalty. And Vince Means prized loyalty above everything, if his ex-wife was right in her assessment. So if Vince was going to hire a killer, he'd want someone whose loyalty could never be in doubt. Someone already tied tightly to him.

Getting a birds-eye view on his entanglements might turn up someone I hadn't considered yet. At the same time, I'd be able to satisfy my curiosity about Dinah Mercer and her museum plans.

My shift ended at two in the afternoon, and I waved farewell to Luanne as I walked out the green doors. She didn't acknowledge me, but her eyes did follow me like a painting in one of those wacky haunted house movies from the sixties. I had yet to find a way to win over the head librarian's heart, but I was committed to keep trying.

I hadn't set foot in the hallowed halls of City Hall yet, but although the exterior was imposing gray stone, the inside was really rather pedestrian. It didn't take long to find the Records Clerk office on the second floor. The clerk on duty was a pleasant young woman in a long skirt and a blouse with lace ruffles down the front. I still couldn't understand how folks could wear such pristine outfits in this humidity and look so put together while I wilted like a chef's salad under a heat lamp.

I approached the desk with a polite smile. "Hi there. I'm the new assistant librarian, and we're planning a town history exhibit at the library next month. I wonder if you could give me access to the town's records so I can get an idea of what to pull together for the exhibit."

She seemed thrilled just to have someone to talk to, let alone someone who showed an interest in the records that were her sacred charge. She took me into the records room, gave me a short tour, and then turned me loose.

I spent an hour digging through records, trying to make heads or tail of what I was reading. I stumbled upon a trove of Means family information, a little amazed that there was so little oversight of these documents. Birth certificates, marriage certificates, property title transfers. The records stretched back for over a hundred years. The most recent ones did not set off any alarm bells as it seemed the Means family had been gradually contracting. There were only a handful of relatives left.

Two were his aunts, both around Miss Dottie's age and definitely too old to pull off a murder-for-hire caper. One was a female cousin with three children of her own and a schoolteacher husband. And there were two more names on the list, but I couldn't find any other records associated with them, making me assume they'd moved away from St. Dismas Parish.

Still, there was plenty to show me just exactly how much of a man of means Vince was. He owned the refinery, of course, and much of the land around it, including the area around his family mansion. But he also owned several plots that were no longer contiguous to his main consolidation. The trailer park, for instance, although his ownership there had already been established. One that stood out in bright relief for me was the land where Scar's auto garage sat.

Vince Means was Scar's landlord, meaning he likely had a key to the place. Which would have made dumping his dead wife's body there a whole lot easier. I let out a frustrated huff. Knowing what Vince's alibi was for the night of Tabby's death was a puzzle piece I was desperate to have.

Could Scar have been the one Vince trusted with his murder-for-hire plot? He was ex-military, after all, so he wasn't unfamiliar with killing. And the fact that Vince held the deed to his livelihood was a big lever to pull. I immediately switched gears, looking for information on Jeffrey "Scar" Sanders, owner and proprietor of American Auto Garage.

He was in his fifties, born and raised in New Orleans, and a decorated veteran. He also had two children and six grandchildren, and he'd been married to the same woman since the early nineties. The probability of his accepting a job like this from Vince didn't seem very high. Besides, he seemed too smart to leave evidence lying around, like the poorly staged crime scene. A man like Scar would know to sink the body in the swamps and let the gators do the dirty work.

I gagged at that thought and sat down, feeling defeated. I was grasping at straws, missing the key pieces of information that would lead me in the right direction. Who was Vince Means' alibi? Where had the killer gotten the drugs? Why leave the body at the garage? Without the answers to those three central questions, I wasn't sure how I'd ever find the murderer and free Stanley.

I took one last glance at the parish map I'd laid out on one of the tables. I'd marked the areas owned by Vince in pencil, but as I'd gone along, I'd also made note of Mercer properties. They'd become fewer over time, many now lost to history and replaced by a more modern building under a new owner. But the Mercers still owned an office building, the bottom floor of which held Dinah's real estate office, a plantation house about a mile from my own, a stretch of business property a block from Main Street next to the American Auto Garage, currently being rented by a laundromat proprietor, and a parcel of land that abutted the Means' main property.

It was that stretch of land that bothered me. From what I could tell, all that stood there was a small wooden cabin. If this was the place where she planned to build her history museum, no wonder Vince had said he wanted no part.

I pushed the information to the back of my brain because it had no bearing on my current investigation. I needed to get back to those three questions. Out of the three, finding out Vince's alibi for that night seemed most pressing. I left the records room and entered the hallway, heading toward the exit. I was considering going back to the sheriff and either bullying the information out of him or abasing myself and begging for it, when the mayor suddenly came around the corner, accompanied by an attractive well-put-together woman in a tight pencil skirt.

I recognized the mayor from his picture in the library. It hung next to the governor and the President of the United States. Pausing, the mayor fired up the smile I bet he used to win elections. "Hey there," he said, his hand out for shaking. "Who have we got here? I always stop to greet my constituents, especially the pretty ones."

The smile on the face of the woman beside him tightened, and without hesitating, she introduced herself as Gita Clarke, the mayor's assistant.

"Pleasure to meet you both. I'm Jade Hastings, the new assistant librarian. I was just upstairs, getting acquainted with the town and its history."

Mayor Travis Landry ran a hand through his unruly salt and pepper hair. He straightened, and if I didn't know any better, I'd say he sucked in his gut at the same time. "Well, if you have any questions, please don't hesitate to consult me personally, day or night. In fact, we could have dinner some night and I could tell you all about the town's history."

I had to restrain my surprise. Was Mayor Travis flirting with me? "Thank you for the offer. I know your wife actually. Alma is a lovely woman. She's a member of my book club."

Mention of his wife seemed to throw cold water over his libido. "Lovely woman, yes. Do excuse me. I have mayoral duties to attend to." He continued down the hall like a ship that had lost its wind.

"I've got to head back to work anyway," I said to his assistant by way of a farewell, although I didn't mean returning to the library. The investigation was my full-time job. For now, the library was incidental.

Gita's response startled me. "Yes, it must be hard making sure all those books stay in their places." Her smarmy tone was like a slap in the face. She walked past me, nose in the air, and that was when I noticed something.

Gita Clarke's shade of lipstick was the exact same as the one worn by Vince Means' secretary.

CHAPTER 19

Sparky's had a crowd for dinner that night, meaning Char and I had to sit on the same side of the booth to hear each other over the boisterous family at the booth next to ours.

"The mayor's assistant and Vince Means? Really?" Char was squirting ketchup on a burger that looked almost as big as her head.

"The lipstick could be a coincidence, sure, but what if it's not? What if Gita is sleeping with Vince and Mayor Travis? You told me yourself that the mayor was having an affair with his assistant. Could that just be gossip?"

"Not likely," Char said between bites. "Everyone in town knows it's happening, except maybe Alma."

"Yes, and I got a dose of the mayor's charm myself earlier. He invited me to dinner to discuss the town's history."

Char laughed and almost choked. Gulping down half a glass of water, she regained her equilibrium. "Welcome to New Orleans. Ladies drink free. At least, that would be our slogan if Mayor Travis was in charge of it."

I put my head down on the table, ready to surrender to the absurdity that was life in a small southern town. "Who would have thought a quaint small town like New Orleans could have such a tangled web of relationships?"

"I warned you," Char said. "Quaint, we are not."

I raised my head, getting frustrated with all the cheating and lying going on around town. "There's also the guy that Taz saw in the Means' mansion. The one Tabby was presumably sleeping with." I could feel my anger rising. A little too loudly, I blurted, "Is everyone in this crazy town having an affair?"

Unfortunately, I picked the wrong time to lose control over the volume of my voice. A woman in a shapeless gray dress with a white collar and built like an LSU linebacker froze as she crossed in front of our booth. She turned to burn me with her gaze, her face standing out white against the dark scarf covering her hair. A gust of fear went through me.

"Godless!" She pointed a finger at me. "Shouting about infidelity around good Christian families!"

"She's sorry, Sister Agnes." Char tried to come to my rescue, but I think even the unflappable Dr. Rains was intimidated.

"God holds this town in his two pure hands, and I won't have your friend here besmirch it."

"I'm sorry," I stammered. "I meant no disrespect."

"Don't apologize to me, girl," the nun hissed in reply. "Apologize to the Lord, for it's him you've offended."

Char tried for another smile. "Sister, she honestly didn't mean it. She's just a little upset. You see, we were talking about poor Tabby's murder."

Sister Agnes snorted, and for a moment, I thought I saw smoke coming out of her nostrils. "There was nothing 'poor' about that girl, especially after she married Vince Means. She was nothing but trouble since she came out of the womb. And what a womb!"

The nun raised her hand, index finger pointed upward. "Evil ends come to evil doers, and evil seeds from evil plants," she bellowed, loud enough that the tables around us cowered as we did. Then as if she'd said nothing at all, she lowered her hand and glided away, the picture of serenity.

"What in the name of Je—"

"Don't blaspheme, not while she's still in earshot," Char whispered frantically. "She'll come back and call the Devil to drag you down to Hell."

I held my tongue. This was not a woman to trifle with. That was apparent. Even though she was anointed by God, I wouldn't want to run into her in a dark alley.

Char swiveled her head around to make sure we were no longer being observed. "That was Sister Agnes Grace, the Headmistress of Our Lady of Perpetual Help, the local Catholic school that most folks around here send their kids to. She's also a kind of local bogeyman. My grandmother used to tell me to behave or Sister Agnes would creep into my room at night, snatch me out of bed, and take me to the Crossroads to give me to the Devil."

My eyes widened. "Wow. That's a healthy dose of terror for a child."

Char let out a burst of cynical laughter. "Imagine when I was five and I started attending Sister Agnes's school." She shook her head. "When I got older, I began to wonder if Sister Agnes started those bogeywoman rumors herself to keep her students in line, since by the time most of us arrived, we were already conditioned to fear her."

Presley stopped by the table to check on us, then quickly moved on. Looking around the diner, I watched as families and friends shared a meal together. On the surface, it was like any other diner in any other small town. I wondered for a moment if other places were as suffused with secrets as New Orleans. Was this place special, or was I just naïve?

"To answer your question," Char said, pulling my focus back to her, "I'm sure New Orleans has its fair share of sneaking around. But look at the bright side. We only need to concern ourselves with the affairs connected to a horrible murder."

I rolled my eyes at her attempt to make me feel better about the situation. Putting my chin in my hand, I leaned on my elbow and considered the current question. "Could Vince and the Mayor, two married men, each be having an affair with the same woman?"

Char chewed contemplatively. "I suppose it could happen," she said after swallowing.

"A love triangle with the mayor," I said. "That could ruin a man's reputation. Even a rich one."

"The mayor may seem like an ornamental position, especially the way Mayor Travis plays it, but there's enough power in the position to inconvenience a businessman like Vince, if wielded right."

I leaned back, abandoning my plate of cheese fries. "If Tabby found out about the affair with Gita, that could be the leverage she had against Vince."

Char set down her burger to pounce on my fries. "Is that really enough of a threat to resort to murder?"

I groaned, tired of all the speculation. Vince was the only real suspect we had, but even so, there was little that made sense. I watched as Char polished off my fries, fascinated by a new mystery. Where did Char keep her second stomach? I'd never met anyone who could put food away like a frat boy with no ill effects and no spare tire around her middle.

She dabbed her mouth daintily, a contrast to the way she'd attacked the meal, and turned back to me. "We're getting nowhere fast."

Her tone was matter of fact. "All we have is possible suspects and potential motives, but we have no way to connect anyone to the crime. Since Vince is our prime suspect, we need to determine once and for all if he's the one who's responsible for Tabby's demise." She paused to finish her sweet tea, likely for dramatic effect. "We should hit the refinery and do some more digging."

My brow furrowed. "I did that, remember? And it didn't end so well. I doubt Vince is going to be eager to welcome me back."

"You got a valuable clue when you were there, remember? The lipstick stain? We just need to figure out another ruse to get us in the door."

"Vince saw through the last one." He'd known I was after information when I'd come to him with the mobile library idea. "I don't think he'll exactly welcome me back after that."

Char tapped her fingers on the tabletop, her expression thoughtful. "I'm not sure any excuse we come up with isn't going to be met with suspicion. The way things stand, Vince probably wouldn't trust his own mother if she wanted to have a friendly chat."

Assuming he was guilty, Char's point made sense. Vince would be looking to avoid traps, which meant he would see us coming. Anything we made up, he'd doubt. "So maybe we needed to go into it assuming he won't believe our cover story."

Char looked at me, intrigued. "If he doesn't believe our story, why would he even agree to talk to us then?"

"Because he won't be able to resist. We just have to figure out the right cover story to make him want to know what we know, enough to risk a chat."

"But what do we know?" Char countered. "We don't have anything but a few crazy guesses."

"If it's true he's seeing Gita, that could be the angle we're looking for. We claim to be representing the mayor to see if we can flush him out."

"That's not a half-bad idea," Char breathed. "But you're right about your cover being blown already. So it would have to be me who takes the lead."

"I've got it." As I spoke, hope unfurled inside me. "You're there on behalf of Mayor Travis's new health initiative. He's looking for support from local business owners. You name-drop the mayor to see if you can get him to give away anything about Gita and his clandestine relationship."

"If it exists," Char said. "All of this is based purely on the lipstick shade supposition. We could end up emptyhanded again."

That was true. "You're taking the lead, right? So while you're having your chat, I can find a way to snoop around the refinery and see if anyone else might have seen Gita around. That way, if you can't crack Vince, we could find corroboration elsewhere."

"It's not a bad idea. It's not a great idea, either, but let's give it a shot."

Char's lukewarm support was enough for me. Our options were

running out, and if Stanley's case made it to trial soon, we'd lose our opportunity to prove his innocence. "I'll pick you up at the clinic after my shift tomorrow."

"Fine," Char said. "On one condition. You get Miss Sally to make up a whole batch of beignets just for us. I'm going to need a dose of sugary courage before we hit the refinery."

I laughed, unable to help myself. Dr. Charlotte Rains was insisting on loading up on sugar before infiltrating an actual sugar refinery. It was wrong on so many levels.

"I'll call her first thing in the morning," I promised.

CHAPTER 20

We were sitting in reception area of the St. Dismas Sugar Refinery, waiting for Vince's receptionist to return from asking whether her boss was available. She'd recognized me, but her lack of reaction made it clear that Vince hadn't shared what we'd discussed after my last visit.

That gave me hope that our Gita-Vince-Mayor Travis love triangle idea wasn't misplaced. If Vince was having an affair with his receptionist, he might mention that he didn't trust the new assistant librarian. The fact that he hadn't could mean that it was Gita who left those stains, not the receptionist.

Then again, I could be completely in the weeds. I was starting to feel like a conspiracy nut. At least my basement walls weren't lined with newspaper clippings connected by lines of red string.

Not yet anyway.

"You should go now," Char said after we'd been waiting for a moment. "I'll tell her you had to leave. Family emergency."

"Good luck," I said as I stood and headed toward the glass door that separated the reception area from the rest of the plant.

"You too," Char called after me. "I'll meet you at the car. First one to get thrown out is a rotten egg."

Entering the hallway, I looked both ways, trying to determine where each direction would lead. To the left, the hallway led to a red metal door. I noticed a pad next to the door, which likely served as a lock. As I had no card or code with which to open it, I decided to head to the right.

The hallway dead-ended into another junction, and again, I looked left and right. This time, the right side ended in a pair of bathrooms, one for men, the other for women. To the left, I could hear the sound of machinery. To the left I went, walking confidently like I belonged there.

The hallway opened into an area filled with machines, a large conveyer belt running all around and through it. Employees in coveralls stood at their stations, while others crossed back and forth over the concrete floors.

I spotted a woman in an orange jumpsuit and figured she might be a good place to start. Women were often more observant than men, and the fact that she was dressed in orange and not blue set her apart as someone with a specialized function. I headed over to where she stood with a clipboard, observing the floor, and I started out with a friendly wave.

"Hey there," I said, speaking loudly so I could be heard over the noise of the machines. "I'm here on behalf of the Mayor's Office. I wondered if you had a moment to chat."

She never took her eyes off the machines. "Not really."

"Okay, I'll make this quick. We're working on a new initiative and we're trying to get feedback from our constituents. Has anyone mentioned this to you yet?"

"No," she said, her face starting to wrinkle in annoyance.

"You sure? Mayor Travis's assistant, Gita Clarke, has been trying to get the word out. Have you seen Gita around the refinery at all?"

"No," she replied. Then a mischievous grin crept across her face. "But then again, I'm not surprised. It must be hard for her to pull herself out of the mayor's bed."

"Oh my," I said, at a loss for words. "I guess you haven't seen Gita then."

"Nope."

My polite smile was back in place. "Thank you for your time."

I walked away, looking for another employee to approach. I found a couple women at the water fountain and asked them, but neither had seen Gita around either. A young man whose coveralls were tidier than others told me they didn't get many visitors at the refinery, especially someone as well put together as Gita Clarke. For a moment, I thought he might have a crush on the mayor's assistant, but the way he started rhapsodizing about her outfits made me realize it was her clothes he desired, not Gita herself.

I was about to try another area of the plant when I noticed a familiar figure operating one of the machines. He was tall, his coveralls covered in grease spots, and his head crowned with a bush of curly dark hair. This was the man who Tammy had hugged the day I met her at her food cart. It was also the man who'd peeled out of the trailer park in his truck with Tammy hollering after him.

I noticed then that a ball cap sat on top of his machine, and it made the wheels in my mind start to turn. Taz had said that the man in Tabby's house that day had been in coveralls and a ball cap. Tabby's mother had said that Tabby had made a play for her boyfriend. Could it be that the man Tabby was kissing that day was her own mother's boyfriend?

I swallowed, my stomach gurgling at the thought. Maybe this man was the missing link we'd been waiting for. If he was carrying on an affair with Tabby behind both Tammy and Vince's back, he might have some ideas about how she ended up dead.

Or he might have had something to do with it himself.

I took a deep breath and started forward, figuring I had nothing to lose in talking to him. When I got close enough to catch his attention, I waved, making him look up.

His brow furrowed. He looked me up and down, then turned off his machine. "Yeah?"

"Hi, there. I'm Jade, a friend of Tabby's."

Confusion writ large on his face, he shook the hand I offered. "Fuzzy."

"Nice to meet you, Mister, uh, Fuzzy." I pulled my hand back and surreptitiously wiped it on the back of my skirt. "I wondered if I could talk to you for a moment about Tabby?"

Fuzzy frowned, replying in a gruff tone. "I don't know why you wanna talk to me about that girl. I barely knew her."

"Well, you are seeing her mother, right? Tammy Carter."

Nodding, he looked me over again, his eyes holding a lifelessness that should have disturbed me. "Yeah, I see Tammy from time to time."

"So you must have known Tabby more than a little, right?"

"What do you want?" Fuzzy asked, his patience running thin.

I knew I wouldn't keep his attention for much longer, so I decided to take a calculated risk. We were at his place of employment, after all, with his coworkers buzzing all around us. It should be safe to ask the question I wanted to know the answer to most.

I leaned in and lowered my voice. "Tabby told me that you two were having an affair."

Fuzzy's eyes widened, and without warning, he grabbed me by the arm, yanking me forward and across the floor to another hallway. I tried to free myself, but his grip was like an iron vise around me.

"Let me go," I said, trying to inject my tone with as much authority as I could muster.

He ignored me, instead shoving me into a storage closet and shutting the door behind us. "Who the heck are you, and what are you trying to do?" he growled when we were alone.

"I told you. I'm Tabby's friend, and I—"

"That girl didn't have any friends." He towered above me, his face turning red, and I felt a ripple of fear roll through me. "Why are you here trying to stir up trouble? You're messing with my livelihood."

I held up my hands, taking a few steps backward until I ran into a shelving unit. "I'm just trying to figure out what happened to Tabby. I want to know the truth."

"Well, I ain't got it," he bit out. "I didn't murder that girl."

"That girl was your girlfriend's daughter. And you were sleeping with her." I was scared, but my anger overcame that fear, the words tumbling out before I could stop them.

"So was half the town!" His leaned in close, and I could see little red veins blooming on the end of his nose. "Tabby liked to push people's buttons. Liked to toy with them. Her mother. Her husband. It was all a game to her. I was just another way for her to score points."

"You didn't mind that she was using you as a pawn? Or maybe you did mind." I tried to stand up to him, tried to hide the fact that he intimidated the heck out of me. "Maybe she threatened you with exposure. To your girlfriend. To your boss. Maybe that's why you did it."

"I didn't do anything," he growled. "I told that girl no when she wanted me to help her rub her husband's nose in her infidelity. She threatened to have her own mama evicted to get back at me."

Tabby was definitely a cold one. Fuzzy lived with her mother. Therefore, to get Fuzzy evicted, she had to get her mother evicted. And she hadn't hesitated.

His voice was like razor wire. "If you're the one thinking about exposing me, I'm not going to stand still and let you screw up my life." He was already crowding me, but now he put his arms up on either side, hands against the shelving unit. I was caged in, trapped.

I tried to reposition myself, tried to shrink into a ball, but when I lifted my left foot to resettle it, I caught it on a stack of shop towels on the bottom shelf and slipped on the fabric. I fell, my butt hitting the floor between Fuzzy's legs.

I wasn't about to let this opportunity go by. As quickly as I could, I scrambled between his legs and back to the door. I pulled myself up and opened it, lunging into the hallway before he could grab me again.

I ran down the hallway, having no idea where I was going other than away from Fuzzy. I could hear his footsteps slamming the floor behind me. He was a big guy and I was a librarian who pathologically avoided cardio, so I knew it was only a matter of time before he overtook me.

Then Vince Means turned the corner, caught sight of me, and let out a yell. "Hey!"

I froze, now trapped between two potential murderers. Fuzzy

slowed to a walk about ten feet behind me. Vince approached, his face heavy with darkness like a storm cloud.

"What are you doing here?" he asked, his voice like gravel. Then a look of realization crossed his face. "You're here with the doctor, aren't you? Like I told her, I know there's no new initiative. You're just trying to snoop."

Out of breath, I started to sputter. "Mr. Means, I was just—"

"You were just leaving, is what you were just doing," he interrupted.

Looking over my shoulder, I saw that Fuzzy was almost close enough to touch. "He—your employee here. Do you know what he and Tabby were—"

Vince looked over my shoulder, then let out a quick laugh. "I don't care if Fuzzy was sleeping with my wife. He wouldn't be the only one. He's a good machinist. I can use that skill way more than I could use a trophy wife who did nothing but lie and cheat on me."

I goggled at the businessman. Surely, not even Vince Means could be this callous. Could he?

"Fuzzy, you get back to work. I'm going to show the librarian out." The man in coveralls did as he was told, burning me with a final blazing look. Vince, his hand on my upper arm, was grumbling as he led me toward the exit.

"I'm giving your description to my security people. If they catch you or the good doctor skulking around here again, I'm going to have you arrested."

He put me out the door, then turned around and left without a backward glance. I made my way to my car, where Char was already waiting for me.

"How'd it go?" she asked me.

"About as well as it went for you."

She nodded. "Let's get out of here. I've already ordered a pizza. Please tell me you have more wine at your place."

Climbing into the car, I let out a shaky breath. "I'm beginning to think that if I'm going to stick around in New Orleans, I better invest in a vineyard."

Char's laughter echoed around the car as we drove out of the refinery's lot.

CHAPTER 21

Chonks was standing on the kitchen table, his demands imperious and urgent.

"I told you I'd be a little late today, Mr. Bossy Pants," I said as I filled his dish.

"He's not in the mood for excuses," Char said with a smile on her face.

"Clearly." I set down the dish in its customary space on the other side of the refrigerator, and Chonks dashed across the table, his steps multiplied as he tried to compensate for the slippery surface. Then he was at his dish, making pig-like grunts as he dug into his dinner.

"A cat after my own heart," Char said as she flipped open the lid on the pizza box. I busied myself with the wine, and soon, we were all settling into our respective poisons of choice.

We'd kept things brief during the car ride, both of us recovering from our adrenaline rushes. I did mention what happened with Fuzzy in the storage closet, and Char had a minor freak-out, offering to give me an examination to see if he'd damaged me in any way.

I convinced her that my butt was big enough to handle the impact and that Fuzzy hadn't gotten a chance to do anything before I made my daring escape. I would live to slip and fall another day.

"So what happened in Vince's office?" I was dying to see if she'd crashed and burned as spectacularly as I had.

"Vince seemed to know I was full of bull from the first words out of my mouth. It sounded convincing as I said it, but almost immediately, he got this smarmy grin on his face, feigning surprise and excitement at everything I said but in an over-the-top way that said he didn't believe a word."

I shook my head, confused. "Are you just a terrible actress? You could have mentioned that fact."

Char stuck her tongue out at me. "I'll have you know that I played Daisy Mae in New Orleans Community Theater's rendition of *Lil Abner*."

"Then how did he know..." I sat back, eyes wide as realization hit me. "He was tipped off."

"What? I mean, how? We're the only ones who knew the plan."

"But we aren't the only ones who would know there is no new health initiative coming out of the mayor's office, right?" I held up my finger, walking through the points as I laid them out. "Say the receptionist comes in and says there's some people from the mayor's office here to see him. Say he is having an affair with Gita. Maybe he wonders what the deal is, so he calls her before you come in. Gita would tell him there was no initiative, and when you come in the room, he already knows you're there under false pretenses."

"Well, I got nowhere quick. He made a few jokes at my expense, let me talk myself in circles, then told me to get the hell out and if I came back again, he'd have my brother arrest me himself."

"Harsh," I set, letting out a long breath. "I didn't do much better. No one I talked to had seen Gita around the refinery. So if she and Vince are having an affair, they're not carrying on at his place of business."

I stared at the slice of pizza on my plate, remembering the mix of fear and excitement I'd felt during our infiltration of St. Dismas Sugar Refinery. Still, we'd gotten little of use out of the adventure.

"He did say he knew about the affair," I murmured to myself.

"Who said? Which affair?"

"Sorry," I said, shaking my head to clear it. "Vince. He said he didn't care if Tabby was sleeping with her mother's boyfriend. In fact, Fuzzy was too valuable of an employee to fire over it, if you believe that."

"Then it's clear Vince didn't have Tabby killed out of revenge for cheating on him." Char frowned. "So we're back to Tabby holding something over Vince's head, like a relationship with the mayor's mistress."

"And we have no evidence for that except for Tammy's word." My brow furrowed. "Maybe Tammy did it."

"Murdered her own daughter?" Char sounded skeptical. "I mean, she's definitely got a crazy streak, but killing her own daughter? Do you think she could do it?"

At this point, I had no idea. We were quickly running out of options. I was never more certain that I wasn't cut out for solving mysteries. "I don't know, but we know she said she'd put Tabby out of the house for messing around with Fuzzy. Assumedly, she meant years ago, since Tabby hasn't lived at home for a while, right?"

Char nodded. "She lived with Vince."

"Where Tabby was still carrying on with Fuzzy. Maybe Tammy found out they were continuing their affair behind her back, got mad, and took matters into her own hands."

Char tossed the crust of her slice of pizza back into the box. "She's a tough woman, but murder? She might love the guy, but it's her daughter."

"There's the eviction too," I added. "Tabby wanted leverage against Fuzzy to make him cooperate, so she threatened to evict her mother, whom Fuzzy lives with. What if Tammy found out about it, and it shoved her over the edge? Tabby could effectively ruin her mother's life. She could steal her boyfriend, kick her out of her home, and probably get Vince to not let her bring her food truck around."

"So Tammy resented her daughter's power over her and did something about it. That's our working theory?"

I nodded.

"It's dark," Char said, pushing the pizza box away. I knew it had to be bad if it was able to kill her endless appetite. "I'm going to head home and try to get some sleep."

"Wanna hit the bazaar tomorrow? Grab some of those apple fritters for breakfast before figuring out our next step?"

Char nodded, but her normal enthusiasm for the fritters was subdued. "See you at ten."

The next morning saw us sitting in the food court area of the bazaar in white folding chairs at a small, perpetually sticky folding table. Armed with apple fritters and cups of chicory coffee, we were going over our options.

I felt deflated, defeated, and by Char's expression, she felt similarly. "We could go back to the trailer park and talk to Tammy again," she said.

"I don't relish another run-in with Fuzzy, especially on his turf."

Nodding, Char set down her fritter. "Honestly, I don't know what good another chat with Tammy would do. She doesn't seem like the type to break down when confronted with her crime."

"Yeah. If you're able to murder your own daughter in cold blood, I doubt the two of us are going to be able to intimidate her into a confession."

We sat there, twin frowns on our faces, silently contemplating the reality of the situation. *We might not be able to free him. Taz will go down for a murder he didn't commit because we will have failed him.*

"What do we have here, two Sad Sallys?" I looked over to where Dottie Turleigh was holding a tomato plant snug against her side. "What's gotten into you ladies? Why so doom and gloom?"

"We've been trying to find Tabby's real killer, and we're coming up empty," Char admitted.

Dottie set her plant on the table, a confused expression on her face. "What do you mean, real killer? Didn't your brother already do that?"

"He's got the wrong man," I said. "Taz couldn't have done this."

"And why not? You know he spent some time in a mental institution, right?"

Both Char and I shook our heads.

"What are you talking about?" Char asked. "I've never heard that before."

Dottie smiled widely and took a seat, primly folding her hands in her lap. Although she looked like the picture of a sweet old Sunday School teacher, she prepared to spill the tea like a pro.

"It was years ago, when the boy was still in high school. His mother told everyone he was in summer camp, but I discovered he was really in an institution in Baton Rouge. I found out when I saw an envelope addressed to his mother Wanda when I was visiting with the postman. You remember Postman Rick, don't you, Char? Such a nice man."

"He was a worse gossip than you are," Char said.

Dottie clutched her pearls, pretending to be scandalized for a second, but she was quick to pick up the thread. "The envelope was from Priory Psychiatric Hospital. Postman Rick said she got one every couple weeks. Probably a bill of some kind."

"Thank you for your opinion, Miss Dottie," Char said, her tone dismissive.

Dottie stood up and sniffed, picking up her plant before sticking out her chin and addressing Char. "Why don't you let your brother do his job? That boy has a dark past. Mark my words."

She walked away, and Char shook her head about the old busybody. "She was probably digging through the mail herself. Postman Rick indeed. He had a belly so big, it would bounce when he'd walk up your steps to drop off the mail. Plus, he would stop and chat to anyone he came across, whether that person wanted a chat or not. It took until seven o'clock somedays before he'd finish his rounds."

"Even if it's true, it doesn't mean Stanley's a murderer." Still, I was rattled by Dottie's intimation.

Before Char could respond, her phone started to ring. She picked it up, then stood up immediately. "I'm on my way. Don't move him." Hanging up, she said she had to run. It was Dr. Loomis's wife. "The old guy slipped and fell, and she's afraid he's broken his hips. Maybe he'll finally retire and take it easy like he should, for his own good."

"You're forgetting your fritter," I called as she started away from the table.

"Wrap it up for me!" she hollered back, then took off at a jog toward the parking lot.

I sat there for a few minutes longer, debating. I was trying to help Stanley, but it was clear I didn't have all the facts. I thought that perhaps it was time to pay a visit to Stanley's mother, to see if what Dottie said was true.

It was a risk. If Sheriff Rains heard I was snooping that close to home, so to speak, he might not view it too kindly. Still, I had to chance it. I had to know why she'd institutionalized her son and determine what it meant for the case.

CHAPTER 22

I pulled up in front of a neat house on the outskirts of town. It was small, nothing more than a square with some windows and a roof, but the lawn was well kept and tidy. Knocking on the door, I wondered if I really had it in me to ask the questions I was about to ask.

It was an invasion of privacy, no doubt about it, but I still believed that Taz was wrongly accused. To be able to counter Sheriff Rains' story, I needed all the information he had. And clearly, he'd found out about Stanley's stay in the Baton Rouge psychiatric hospital.

The door opened, exposing a middle-aged woman in an apron with a question mark on her face.

"Hi," I said, introducing myself. "I'm the new assistant librarian and a friend of your son. Can I come in?"

For a moment, I thought she was going to say no, but she finally moved aside to let me enter. As we walked to the back of the house, I realized that Taz and his mother didn't have much money. I could have fit their entire house, furniture and all, into the blue sitting room in my plantation house.

Once we were settled at the kitchen table, I let her know why I was there. "Mrs. Lane, I've only recently moved to New Orleans, but in that time, I've struck up a friendship with Stanley. He's incredibly bright, and he might love books even more than I do."

"Call me Wanda," she said, visibly softening when I talked about her son. "Stanley always loved his books."

"I've tried talking to Sheriff Rains, tried convincing him that your son wasn't involved, but so far, it has fallen on deaf ears."

Wanda nodded, and I could see her becoming emotional. "I said the same thing. My boy wouldn't do something like that, even to that wicked girl. The sheriff told me they had evidence, even asked me about that night."

"What did you tell him?"

"I had to tell the truth," Wanda said. "He came home late with no shirt on, the dirt from the road sticking to his sweat."

"Did Stanley tell you what happened that night?"

Wanda shook her head, then let out a large sniffle. "He rarely talks to me or anybody. That night was no different. I asked him what happened when he came in, but he said nothing, just got in the shower, then went straight to bed."

"You don't know what he was doing? Who he was with?"

"No more than you do." Her voice had a little edge. She was getting defensive. I couldn't blame her, and I didn't want to put up any walls between us before I got into the real reason I was there.

"Mrs. Lane—Wanda—I really hate to ask this. I'm not usually one to pry, but I've been trying to find out who could have killed Tabby. I've come up with a list of suspects, but I haven't been able to find any evidence that clears your son. And I've just come across a piece of information that could make things even harder."

Her expression was neutral, but there was a hint of anxiety in her eyes. It was like she already knew what I was going to ask. I tried to phrase it carefully to show that I understood how delicate the issue was. "I recently learned that Stanley may have struggled with some... emotional issues... when he was younger. I wondered if your son has been diagnosed with anything that could have been used as an excuse to pin this crime on him."

Wanda stared down at the tabletop, unconsciously straightening the lace. She took a long, slow breath. "Stanley was in an institution, back when he was in high school. Not many people know because I told everyone he'd gone away to summer camp up north, but you can never keep anything completely a secret in a small town like New Orleans."

"What was wrong with Stanley?" I asked, not liking the way I'd phrased the question but not able to think of a better way of asking. "Did something happen to him?"

"Post traumatic stress disorder," Wanda whispered, her fingernail tracing the swirls in the lace. "Stanley was a good boy, if always a bit quiet and introverted. A counselor in grade school said he might be on the spectrum. People down here don't exactly understand a thing like that. Mostly, they just thought he was odd. But it got worse in high school."

I kept myself from responding, waiting for the story to come out of her, bit by bit.

"It was my fault," she said finally on a sob. "My husband wasn't a nice man. Oh hell, I'll just come out and say it. He was a brutal dictator who used violence to control us." She looked me in the eye for the first time in several minutes. "I've been doing a lot of reading about abusive relationships. I'm trying."

I nodded, my expression encouraging her to continue.

"Although I bore the brunt of my husband's anger, Stanley wasn't immune. His father wasn't shy about using his fists on a child, sadly."

"Did you put him in the institution because of something his father did to him?" The thought of a young Taz being physically abused by a grown man made me sick to my stomach.

"Not exactly. Maybe indirectly. Not long after Stanley turned fifteen, his father disappeared. Went on a run to the liquor store and just never came back."

She looked at me, her eyes wet with tears. "At first I thought it was a good thing. I never had the strength to throw him out, but at least he was gone. Then my son started having nightmares. Bad ones. 'Night terrors' his doctor called them later. He would wake up screaming, over and over, all night long. I didn't know what to do."

She wiped at her eyes, sniffling. "I took him to Dr. Loomis, and Loomis suggested the hospital in Baton Rouge. I didn't know what else to do. I just knew things couldn't go on the way they were. So I committed him."

I couldn't imagine how hard that decision must have been. "Did you visit him there?"

"As often as I could. Every weekend for certain."

"How was he reacting to the hospital?" I wondered how a bright boy like Stanley would have adapted to an institutional setting.

"Better than I expected. Taz wasn't a boy to easily make friends, but he seemed to be getting along with his doctors, and they were impressed with him and his progress. His nurse said he was the best behaved patient she'd ever had." I noted the hint of pride in her tone.

"He came home just before school started, and he was sleeping through the night. Post traumatic stress. That's what the doctors said had triggered the night terrors. He was no longer scared of his father's beatings. He was afraid that his father would come back."

Her voice breaking, she continued. "The beatings, as the doctors explained it, were a known thing. Expected. Something he could deal with. But with his father gone, all that was left was uncertainty. The beatings were gone but not forgotten, and Stanley lived in fear of the day his father would come back."

I put my arm on her back, my heart breaking for her and her son. "I'm sorry, Wanda. That must have been so difficult."

"I shouldn't have put my son through that for so long. The guilt that hit me then, knowing that he was more afraid of *not* getting hit?" Breaking down, she put her head on her arms that were crossed on the tabletop.

I dug in my purse, coming out with a plastic envelope of tissues. "Here," I whispered, passing the tissues her way. "I know this is very hard."

"People talk," she said. "I know my boy is different, but he's a good boy."

"He is. And PTSD isn't a terrible diagnosis, although it could be misinterpreted." I took Wanda's hand and squeezed it. "Thank you for talking to me today. I'm going to do what I can to bring Stanley home."

She walked me to the door, slowly getting a handle on her emotions. "I'm glad Stanley has a friend like you."

I couldn't help myself. I hugged her tightly and promised to find the real killer. Part of me knew I was hugging her because I couldn't hug Stanley. He must be so scared in that cell, knowing he was going to jail for something he didn't do.

As I left, I noticed my car was almost on empty. I remembered that Pop's gas station wasn't far from where I was, so I headed in that direction. The sun had gone down in the time I was with Wanda, but the lights at the station were still brightly lit. I pulled up to a pump and climbed out of my car, noticing the old man sitting on the wooden chair outside the station's front window.

I usually got gas at the more modern station on the north end of town, just past the city limits. The pumps here were old, the kind that didn't have credit card readers built in. I walked toward the old man, assuming this was Pops.

"Can I get a fill-up?" I asked, pulling out my card.

Pops pulled himself slowly out of his chair, and it looked like he'd stopped halfway, his stoop was so pronounced. I followed him inside, the must of ages hitting me like a wall. Wrinkling my nose, I hoped the transaction would be quick, but as the internet signals in New Orleans were as weak as my desire to have a balanced diet, that wasn't likely. It took long enough for me to pull a tissue out of my purse and press it to my nose as an extra line of defense.

He finally handed me back my card, along with a receipt that looked like it was in hieroglyphics. I headed back to my car and shoved the nozzle into the gas tank, setting the latch on the handle so the gas pumped itself.

I wandered back over to the station's owner. "You're out here pretty late," I said.

He shrugged. "I don't have elsewhere to be, young lady."

"Were you out this late on the night Tabby Means was murdered?"

I already knew he was, according to my conversation with Sheriff Rains, but I figured it was best to start at the beginning.

"Sure was. Later even."

"So you saw them that night? Tabby and Taz?"

He eyed me, then nodded. "Seen a lot of things, that included."

"How could you be sure it was them? That both of them were in the car?"

The corner of Pop's mouth curled up, exposing big yellow teeth that reminded me of a horse. "You doubting my eyesight or my memory, girl?"

"I'm just wondering why you're hanging out here all hours of the day and night. No disrespect, but you're an older gentleman."

He turned his head to the side and spat on the ground. "That's right. I'm an old geezer who ain't got nothing better to do. I only sleep a few hours a night, anyway, so at least this gives me something to do, doesn't it?"

I held up my hands in surrender. "No offense was meant."

He eyed me. "Stayin' open late gives me the opportunity to see strange things from time to time. Like that Carter girl, squealing by in her late-model Mercedes. She's the only one that drives that car, and the only one that drives like that. That's how I knew it was her." He pointed to where they'd passed. "Him, I could see in the passenger side. His head was hanging out the window, almost like a dog's. I think her driving was making him car sick. But I seen him clear as day."

It sounded like Pop's story was solid. Except for one thing. I was returning to my car when I stopped and turned back. "What about on the way back? Who was driving the Mercedes then?"

"Didn't see it. Told Sheriff Rains the same thing. Only saw them going the one way, toward the Means' place."

I heard the pump click, so I headed back to my car, but his words stopped me halfway there. "Saw him coming back, though. Not in the Mercedes this time."

I turned around. "Beg pardon?"

"The weird kid. I saw him walking back later that night. Didn't have a shirt on. I figured it was late enough for me to head home. Figured I'd seen it all by then. Guess I was wrong."

"You saw Stanley walking alone? Why in the heck didn't you tell Sheriff Rains about that part?" I couldn't believe what I was hearing.

Pops scowled. "That dang sheriff. I ain't doing him no favors. He didn't give me no help with those dogs that keep tearing up my fence."

I wanted to throw my hands up in frustration. "But you told him the rest! Why stop there?"

Pop looked down, adopting a mealy-mouth tone. "He didn't ask me. I was telling my story, and he got a call on his radio. Dispatch saying they had some kind of results in. Rains cut me short and took off. And he ain't been back yet."

I put my hand to my forehead. A key piece of evidence had never been revealed because the sheriff had hurt some old guy's feelings. This place couldn't be more absurd if it tried.

"Thank you, Pops," I said, reining in my emotions.

"Happy to help," he said before spitting again.

I climbed in my car, turning over this new piece of information in my head. Pop seeing Taz walking home was big, but it wasn't enough on its own to clear him. I knew I'd only get one shot with Sheriff Rains, and it had to go right.

I needed to connect the dots on my own before bringing them to Rains. It was time to pull out the red string.

CHAPTER 23

The library was the one place in the house I went to for refuge. It calmed me, settled my spirit. Tonight, it wasn't having its usual effect.

I paced the large rug that covered a section of the polished hardwood floor. Going over the clues in my head like they were fine gems I was examining for flaws, I realized I was no longer sure of anyone's motives. The list of suspects, once long, was now nearly a dead end.

Mercy and Jimmy seemed sincere, Fuzzy and Tammy were a long shot, and Vince's hired-killer theory was holding less and less water. It was beyond frustrating to have gone through all this effort, from physical danger to threats of police harassment, not to mention earning the stink eye from Luanne for the times I'd shown up late because of my investigation, and I was still at square one.

I had to focus once again on the facts. Someone killed Tabby with an overdose, then set up the crime scene to make it look like a suicide. This someone had staged the scene at the auto garage, a location chosen for a reason. But figuring out that reason wasn't easy.

By marrying Vince, Tabby had shown she was over her relationship with Jimmy. According to Jimmy himself, it was over between them once Tabby took up with Vince. I thought about Tabby, about her veneer of the happily married woman. She seemed to want people to think she and her husband had a successful marriage. And at the same time, she didn't hide the fact that she was screwing around behind his back.

Tabby had come to that book club meeting because her husband wanted her to. By her own words, she'd wanted some "so-called refinement," at Vince's encouragement. She didn't seem like the type to sit through a book club meeting if she hadn't wanted to impress her husband. Which was at odds with the idea that she was sleeping with half the guys in town.

Maybe Tabby wanted to make their relationship work. A guy like Vince would have insisted on a prenuptial agreement, especially since he was fresh off a divorce. From the treatment Mercy was getting, I figured his prenup with Tabby would be like Louisiana humidity —unbreakable.

The killer had hit on suicide as a way to disguise the death. So why put Tabby at the garage? Whoever had put her there was trying to make the authorities think Tabby chose that place to kill herself. Why would the killer have thought Tabby was motivated to kill herself there?

The staged suicide itself was a red herring laid by the killer. That much was already clear. The murderer could have known the police would see through the staging, which meant they'd put her body at the garage to pin the suspicion on someone specific. Jimmy Beal seemed the most likely person.

And yet Jimmy Beal wasn't the one in jail right now. Taz was. If Jimmy was the intended subject, why leave Taz's shirt at the scene? It didn't make sense.

Chonks let out a meow and I looked down, realizing that he was pacing alongside me. I ignored him, continuing to think in circles. The cat didn't take kindly to being ignored, so he jumped up on one of the shelves behind me, managing to wedge himself between the shelf above and the books below.

Then there was my conversation with Wanda Lane. Taz had spent time in an institution for post traumatic stress disorder. PTSD could bring on depression, anxiety, hostility, and even destructive behavior. Could I be all wrong about Stanley?

I hoped not. After all, he'd been a model patient at the psychiatric hospital. He'd made friends with the staff as well, it seemed. This made me stop in my tracks. Could Taz still be friendly with the folks at the hospital? Is that where the drugs could have come from?

Patrick Mercer had mentioned that a quantity like the one used to kill Tabby was most often used in hospitals and clinics, after all. Maybe Stanley had used his connections at the psychiatric hospital to buy or steal the drugs.

Another yowl from the cat had me rolling my eyes. Seeing that I wasn't moved by his badgering, he stuck a paw out as I passed, latching onto my shirt.

"Come on, Chonks. You're going to claw the fabric all up."

He tried the same trick several times, and I could tell he didn't like my pacing.

"Too bad, Chonks. Until I figure this out, I'm going to wear a hole in this rug."

Chonks looked at me like I was the stubborn one. He sat on the books, his tail swishing with agitation. But annoying my cat was the least of my worries. I paid him no mind, going round and round with myself over the evidence. Why the garage? And how did the T-shirt play into the staging.

Out of the corner of my eye, I saw movement, but it wasn't until I felt an impact on my foot that I realized what was going on. Chonks, in classic cat fashion, had decided to start knocking things off the shelf. I stopped pacing, bending down to pick up his victim.

Turning the book over in my hand, I realized he'd knocked down a copy of *The Great Gatsby*. There were a couple lying around, since I'd brought some home with me from the library in case any book club members neglected to bring their own.

I stared down at the book, considering all that had happened since that first meeting. I'd started the club to do something good for the community, and it had ended up with someone dead. I didn't feel responsible for Tabby's death, but I did mourn for the lost opportunity. I wanted to bring people together. Instead, things were falling apart.

I'd managed to make a few friends in my new town, and they were good ones. Char, for instance, was fast on her way to being the best friend I'd ever had. My life had been a fulfilling but solitary one back in Baltimore, with most of my friends being work colleagues who I didn't see after the library closed. It felt good to have a partner in crime that wasn't four-legged and furry.

But the number of potential enemies I was making far exceeded the handful of people who seemed predisposed to like me. It seemed everywhere I turned, I was stepping on toes. And a few of those toes belonged on powerful feet. If the people of New Orleans decided to hold a grudge, I might never be accepted in my new hometown. For someone who'd set out to help build community, I sure had managed to screw it up royally.

Maybe I could reinvent myself, like Gatsby had. He'd had a war to work with, though. I wasn't sure what kind of re-branding I could manage that would make the residents of New Orleans flock to my house for legendary social events. Maybe I should consult Dinah on that one.

While I was on the subject of Dinah Mercer, I wondered what category she fit in. Not a friend, really, but so far, she didn't seem like an enemy. Just a very determined historical society president. Maybe Dinah was right in a way. Maybe this was too much house for me.

More like too much town for me. Apparently, size wasn't the sole determination of the level of chaos that could befall a municipality. I could cut ties. Sell the house and make amends with Uncle Mike's memory.

As much sense as that might make, the truth was I liked New Orleans. Sure, I wasn't thrilled with its secrets, and some of its inhabitants might make me cringe, but overall, it was a nice place to live. I felt more at home here than I had ever felt in the big city.

Still, if Stanley ended up convicted for this crime, I wasn't sure if I could live with myself or the town anymore. A perversion of justice on that scale was just too unacceptable. Having to see the look on Wanda's face every time I ran into her at the Tip Top or Pop's gas station, it would kill me. Knowing that I failed her son would haunt me. So would the fact that a murderer was still walking free among us.

I shivered at that thought, bringing my focus back to the book cover. The pair of bright floating eyes stared back at me over the lights of the city. I knew that the cover art was meant to reference the billboard mentioned in the book. The eyes of a long-dead doctor keeping eternal watch over an ash heap.

It hit me suddenly what the eyes reminded me of. The faded ad for reading glasses, sitting in Mercer Drug, looked surprisingly similar. They stared with their sightless gaze at the world before them, brooding over the ebb and flow of the town's currents. They could watch, but they couldn't affect those they watched over.

Be it the valley of ash or the sultry streets of New Orleans, Louisiana, the eyes could keep their vigil, but fate still played itself out as written. The parallel was a little jarring, so I sat down to clear my head.

Returning to the investigation, I again reminded myself of the basic facts. Despite the staging, the truth was that Tabby Means died of an overdose. I'd tried once to chat with Patirck Mercer about where those drugs could have come from, but he'd tightened up quicker than a virgin with a hand on her knee. At the time, I'd assumed he'd taken offense at being considered a possible avenue for drugs that had been used to murder someone.

But as I considered it now, why wouldn't he be considered? As Char had said when Chonks used her pill bottle for a toy, most everyone in town got their prescriptions filled through Mercer. Of course, he'd be the first one the cops would question about a controlled substance, right? Then why was he so defensive?

I looked at the intricate glass-domed clock on the mantelpiece and realized I had a little time before the drug store closed. I could get down there just before Mercer locked the doors and have a little chat with the pharmacist. If he had nothing to do with the drugs that killed Tabby Means, then he should have no reason to worry.

Really, I was the one who should worry. If I burned my bridges with Mercer and I was wrong, I'd be driving all the way to Laplace to fill my prescriptions from now on.

CHAPTER 24

I stood in front of the giant eyes, so like Dr. T.J. Eckleburg's, and wondered what they'd seen. The drug store would be closing soon, and through the large glass fronts, I could see that it was already empty of customers. Patrick stood behind the pharmacy counter, his back to the street, presumably counting out pills and placing them into their containers.

The streetlights began to flash on around me, causing me to glance down the street. I saw the laundromat across the street from Mercer Drug and, at the end of the block, American Auto Garage. I remembered then who owned each property. Mercer and Means, Means and Mercer, their marks on each property like invisible flags claiming territory. The whole town could practically be divided up that way.

I shivered, even though I wasn't in the slightest bit cold, and pulled open the door and went inside. Patrick looked over his shoulder when he saw me enter, then quickly turned back to the task at hand. I wandered aimlessly down the aisles, building up the courage to have what my mother might have called "a difficult conversation." That usually described a discussion of why I wasn't dating or whether I saw grandchildren in her future. The conversation currently in the offering was darker but no less fraught with danger.

I was considering the claims on the back of a bottle of lotion when a voice came from over my shoulder. "I'm closing in about five minutes."

I jumped in surprise, then laughed nervously. Putting the bottle back on the shelf, I turned around. "Actually, could you help me with something? I can't sleep, and I'm hoping you can recommend something."

"Follow me," he said, his earlier friendliness absent. Patrick apparently was no longer fond of the town's new assistant librarian. He led me to a shelf with a multitude of sleep aids. I looked at a couple, then frowned.

"Are these the strongest you have? You see, I suffer from pretty acute insomnia and I haven't gotten barely any sleep for days. I had a prescription back in Baltimore, but it's expired now and I've yet to see a doctor since I got to New Orleans."

Patrick frowned. "You could probably call your doctor, get one last renewal on your current script."

"She's on vacation," I said, improvising. "Europe. Won't be back for several weeks."

"Then I suggest you go see Charlotte Rains at her clinic. She'll likely prescribe something for you."

I made a pout. "You see, Dr. Rains and I sort of have a little misunderstanding. Long story short, she won't see me as a client."

It was clear Patrick was quickly losing patience with my plight. "Then you'll have to see a doctor in the next town over. All I have is what's on the shelf, and I'm about to close, so please make your choice."

"None of these will work," I whined. "And I'm sooo tired. Do you know what it's like not to be able to sleep?" I moved closer and started wheedling. "I know you have stronger stuff in the back. All I want it a couple pills, just for tonight. I swear I won't tell a soul."

"I could lose my license," he growled. "Stronger medication is strictly controlled."

"They'll never find out," I countered. "Just two pills? In all the thousands you deal with every week?"

"I have to keep a strict inventory. If anything is missing, I have to account for it if there's an audit. Even if it's just two."

I tried to keep hidden my excitement as Patrick followed me down the garden path, right to where I had a bear trap hidden among the flowers. "If that's the case, then how long will it be before the authorities figure out that the medication used to kill Tabby Means came from your pharmacy?"

I knew it was a longshot, but it was the only shot I had. It was a classic blindside, and for a moment, I thought I'd failed, but then I saw his face crumble.

"How did you find out? Did she tell you?"

"It wasn't hard to figure it out." I jerked my thumb at the front door. "Why don't you lock up and turn off the sign? Wouldn't want anyone disturbing us, would we?"

Patrick did as I suggested, shoulders slumped and face a mask of despair. When he'd locked up behind us, I asked him what prompted him to participate in a heinous murder.

"It never started like that," he protested, his face full of alarm. "When she first came to me with the idea of convincing Means to sell, I thought it was a good one."

He'd yet to tell me who the "she" he was talking about was, but I wasn't about to interrupt him now. It was clear that Means was somehow involved but wasn't the main character. Which meant Vince hadn't killed his wife after all.

"If the thing went off like she said it would and tourists started flocking to New Orleans, then I'd stand to make some money too. I've already got plenty of inventory that would sell well with that kind of crowd. If she could get the lot at the end of the block, I knew she'd turn it into something special."

My eyes widened as I suddenly understood what Patrick was talking about. "The museum. Of course."

He nodded. "But Vince wouldn't sell, and he made darn sure everyone knew it at the Papa Noel ceremony. Dinah got upset, and she got to where she couldn't sleep at night, or so she said. She came to me, saying she needed something to knock her out at night. Dr.

Loomis wasn't taking her seriously, so could I get her something stronger?"

"I told her what I told you, and she said she understood. Then she asked me what I would prescribe so she could go back and argue some more with Dr. Loomis. I told her about the liquid benzodiazepine, saying she wouldn't need too much and she could mix it in with some juice rather than swallow a bunch of pills."

He looked out over the quiet street and frowned. "I figured I'd heard the end of it, that Dinah had given up on her dream, but I was doing a monthly inventory on my stock recently and that's when I noticed I was missing something. A big bottle of liquid benzodiazepine. The dosage was so big, I only stocked it for the local hospital in case they somehow maxed out their supply."

"You think Dinah took it?"

I could tell he didn't want to say, but he finally nodded. "She's my cousin, and this is one of the buildings that's been in our family for generations. I know she has a key somewhere. She's got keys to a lot of the historical properties around town, it turns out. I saw the ring once in her purse when she was digging for one of her business cards. I asked her about it, and she blew me off, saying something about the purview of the president of the historical society."

He gestured to the wall where a small white box with a gray keypad set. "If she had the key, it would have been easy enough to find out the combination for the alarm. All she'd have to do is watch me set it."

I was quickly coming to grips with what had been revealed. Dinah Mercer took the benzodiazepine. Did that mean she also killed Tabby Means? But why?

"You have to go to the police," I told him.

Patrick hung his head. "I know. When I found out about Tabby, I felt so bad I almost turned myself in then. But I didn't want to lose my business if the city decided I was an accomplice. I've built this drug store up all on my own, and I'd even had plans for an expansion if the historical museum brought in enough tourist dollars."

I watched as he heaved a sigh, genuinely upset at the turn of events.

"I realize that it must be disappointing to lose out on your dream of selling joke hats to folks on summer vacation, but a woman is dead because of your cousin's hare-brained scheme."

Guilt made him green at the gills. "I know. And I'm ready to confess my part in this."

"Good."

I knew I was on my way to freeing Taz, but I still wasn't sure our case was strong enough. We could postulate that Dinah stole the drugs from Patrick's pharmacy, but could we somehow connect her to the crime itself? That was the next necessary step if Rains was going to believe that someone other than Taz killed Tabby.

"I will meet you at the police station," I told Patrick. "I just have to make a quick stop first." I made it to the door and waited for him to unlock it. As I was making an exit, I turned back to him. "And if you think you can just change your mind and sweep this under the rug, think again. I'll make sure to hold you accountable."

"I'll be there," he said, his face belonging to a defeated man.

I hopped into my car, even though I was only going a few blocks. As I pulled away from the curb, the eyes of Mercer Drug watched over me.

CHAPTER 25

I knew that it was after hours for City Hall, but often, government functionaries weren't always out of their offices on time. I figured if I could find a way in, I could make it to the records room and grab a few choice items with which to make my case with Sheriff Rains. It wasn't even half past five yet, which gave me a good chance of finding an opening.

The big front doors were locked, but I knew that every side of the square building had an entrance. It was on the back side that I found an unlocked door and let myself inside.

As I made my way up the stairs, I went over what I'd just learned. Dinah Mercer, the woman obsessed with preserving New Orleans's storied past, might have gone as far as murder to accomplish her goal.

She'd been pushing for a historical museum, and I had envisioned some lovingly restored historical property, some plantation house with stately columns that she would fill with period pieces and small lettered signs proclaiming the year each object had been made. But if that were the case, why not use her own house? That was a property she already owned. Instead, she'd been planning something at least in part on a property owned by Means.

I assumed it would be one of the properties that adjoined, but something Patrick had mentioned was tripping me up. He'd said "the lot at the end of the block." That meant I was looking for a plot that was at the end of a block of city street or even county road.

And then there was the matter of Dinah's keyring. Patrick said she had a ring chock full of keys. I considered her role as both president of the historical preservation society and as the lead realtor in the parish. If she made copies of any keys given to her while selling a house or inspecting a property for historical certification, she could have entry into half the buildings in New Orleans.

It was another reason to pull the paperwork. If I could figure out what property Dinah had her eye on for the museum, I might be able to determine whether she had keys to other properties—properties owned by Vince Means.

Reaching the entrance to the Records Office, I turned the knob, but it didn't budge. The office was locked. I tried jiggling the knob just in case it was stuck but had no luck. Turning around, I leaned my back against the door, head touching the frosted glass, and let out a long sigh.

I needed something to bolster the case against Dinah Mercer. Patrick's testimony was damning, but the more threads tying her to the murder, the better. I wanted the property maps and titles to show the scope of Dinah's plan and speak to her motive. It might not be a smoking gun, but it would at least show that she could benefit from the Means tragedy.

But if Dinah was determined to get a plot of land off Vince, why kill Tabby? The question struck me suddenly, and I wanted to groan in frustration. I felt like I was so close to unraveling the mystery. There was just one piece that wasn't clear.

What did Tabby have to do with Dinah's beef with Vince? Why murder her when it was unlikely she'd be able to affect the property transfer anyway?

I was so lost in thought that I didn't hear the clack-clack-clack of Gita's heels as she approached. Her voice pulled me out of my reverie. "I know what you're trying to do."

I turned, surprised at the look of hatred on her otherwise beautiful face. "Beg pardon?"

"You and Dr. Rains and your ridiculous little scheme. I know what you're doing, and it's not going to work."

I frowned, confused. "Look, Ms. Clarke. I'm not sure what you're talking about but I can assure you that—"

"No. Let me be the one that assures *you*." She stepped closer, pressing her index finger, topped by a blood-red fingernail, into my chest. "I'm on to you. You need to back off, or you will regret it."

I was no longer in the mood to play nice. I needed to get back to the police station. "Look, I don't have time for your games. I'm trying to aid in a police investigation. You can do me a favor and unlock this door, or you can leave me alone."

She looked at me like I'd slapped her. "Aren't you a piece of work? I don't know who you think you are, but let me remind you of your place." She looked me up and down, hostility radiating out of her small perfect pores. "You're a librarian, a nobody, just a mousy overgrown girl who needs to go home and let the grownups go about their business."

"Sure, whatever," I said, waving away her insults. "If you're not going to open the door, then you'll have to excuse me."

I pushed past her, causing her to exclaim in surprise. She wasn't caught off guard for long however. Her heels clicked after me, her tone harsh. "You don't get to dismiss me! We aren't done here."

"What do you want, Gita?" I asked over my shoulder as I kept walking. "I'm busy."

"I told you what I want. Leave Vince alone."

I stopped, the realization that I was right about Gita and Vince's secret hitting me. "You're having an affair with Vince Means."

"And that means you're going to back off and keep your little kitten claws out of my man."

"I'm not interested in Vince," I said. "I'm just trying to find Tabby's killer."

Gita rolled her eyes. "Yeah. Sure. And I love posing for pictures with Travis's fish after he pulls them out of the river. We both have to maintain appearances. But I can see through your little cover story. You barely know Taz, and the only person you seem to be questioning is Vince."

"That's because his wife was the one who was murdered!" I was becoming exasperated at Gita's insistence that I was interested in Vince romantically. "He's a prime suspect."

A sudden thought hit me. Maybe Vince wasn't the prime suspect. Maybe it was the woman in front of me, the one warning me away from the man she wanted. Could she have decided she wanted Tammy out of the way? Maybe Dinah was only the conduit, and she turned the drugs over to Gita to carry out her jealous scheme.

"No, he's not," she hissed. "Who do you think he was with that night, dummy?"

"Of course," I said, Vince's alibi finally revealed. "He was with you."

And just like that, I eliminated Gita from the suspect list. She was with Vince, and unless Vince and Gita had acted together in coordination with Dinah, then they hadn't killed Tabby. Besides, Gita seemed more like a spider that waited to trap her prey. She hadn't gone after Mercy when she was married to Vince, after all.

Even if Tabby had found out about the affair between her husband and Gita, the worst she could do was tell Mayor Travis. And if Gita planned to marry Vince, then that secret was bound to come out anyway. No, Gita wasn't Tabby's killer. She was just a run-of-the-mill homewrecker.

Gita nodded. "Sheriff Rains knows it, and now you do too. So you can stop showing up at his office with your little mobile library and your fake mayoral initiatives. Vince isn't interested in you."

"Thank God for small favors," I murmured. "But while you're busy laying your claim on Vince, I have to wonder, does Mayor Travis know? Isn't he your beau too?"

Scowling, Gita brandished her finger again. "Mind your own business, Librarian. You're not going to make any friends in this town by sticking your nose into everything."

"Agree to disagree," I replied, knowing I was cementing friendships by helping Stanley. "Let me just put your worries to rest. I'm not interested in Vince Means."

"Good. Because he's mine. He's finally single again, and this time, no young tramp is going to get in my way. I'm going to be the next Mrs. Vince Means."

"You're welcome to the title," I said. "Best of luck, since it doesn't seem to have worked out so well for the other women who have held it."

Gita gave me a look that would have turned me to cinders if she'd had her way. She stalked off, heels clicking, leaving me at the top of the stairs that led back to the entrance I'd come in through.

I hesitated, debating what to do next. Patrick was likely at the sheriff's office by now, revealing everything to Rains and his men. I needed to be there to make sure I could help Rains and his team connect the dots. But I still lacked a means of connecting Dinah to the crime, beyond her likely theft of the drugs used to kill Tammy.

Then it hit me. I might have the ability to link her to the crime scene already in my possession. It would require a detour, delaying my arrival at the sheriff's office, but if it proved to be the smoking gun to connect Dinah without a doubt to the crime she committed, then I had no choice but to go after it.

I raced down the steps, hoping against hope Chonks hadn't destroyed the evidence already.

CHAPTER 26

The plantation house was dark, save for the light I always left on in the front parlor in case I came home after dark. I let myself in, expecting to find Chonks in the hall. His dinner was late, and I was expecting him to give me hell over it, but this time, the sound of my key in the lock failed to bring him running down the hallway.

Shutting the door behind me, I headed toward the library, the last known location of Dinah Mercer's business card. She'd given it to me, telling me to call if I wanted to sell my house to her. Now I was going to use it to lock her away if possible.

If Sheriff Rains could get a good print off the business card, he could match it to any prints found at the crime scene. My guess was he'd find Dinah's prints in Tabby's car and at the auto garage.

I stood in the middle of the room, trying to remember where I'd stuck the card, when I heard a noise, almost like the squeak of door hinges. I was alone, so I chalked it up to the mystery sound that still haunted my nights. I'd yet to locate its source, but I'd been distracted by my investigation lately, so I hadn't put much effort into it, despite my desire for another visit from the handsome handyman.

I remembered pulling Dinah's card out of the litter box and

sticking it in a copy of *The Great Gatsby*. But which copy? And where had I put it?

I picked up the nearest copy, the one Chonks had tossed on my foot, and paged through it, but there was no card inside it. I located another copy and grabbed a cover in each hand, spreading the book open and shaking it, hoping a card would fall out.

None did.

I cursed under my breath, wondering why I hadn't stuck the card somewhere more secure. Forcing myself to think hard, I remembered that the card wasn't the only thing Dinah had given me. I also had the map. Char and I had spent some time looking it over, so I knew our fingerprints would be on it as well, but maybe Rains could still pull a clean print off the map if I couldn't locate the car.

I saw another copy of *Gatsby* on the long table behind the sofa. Snatching it up, I shuffled through the pages, hoping this was the correct copy.

Suddenly, a yowl sounded in the hall, and I heard the rush of little cat feet. Chonks burst into the library, meowing frantically at me. He stood on his back legs, reaching up at me, his claws sinking through the thin material of my slacks and hooking into flesh.

I bit back a cry of pain and bent down, gently removing his claws from my leg. "What's going on, Chonks? Did you finally remember I hadn't fed you yet?"

Chonks ran in circles, his mewling urgent. This wasn't his typical annoyed "feed me" protests. Something was wrong.

"Chonks, are you—"

I heard a noise behind me and my heart jumped into my throat. The sound was too close to be made by the "ghost" in my walls. I turned just in time to see Dinah rushing toward me, a needle in her hand.

I did the only thing I could think of. I threw the copy of *Gatsby* at her head.

Dinah blocked it with her other arm, and then she was on me, shoving the needle deep into my arm.

I fell backward against the table, letting out a shout that was more fright than pain. Almost immediately, I felt weak. Whatever was in the needle Dinah put in my arm was having an effect, and fast.

My knees buckled and I fell to the floor, landing on my stomach. Still, I wasn't willing to give up. It was clear now that Dinah was a cold-blooded murderer, which meant I had to get away or risk ending up like Tabby Means.

I started to crawl across the floor, pulling myself forward, my muscles an uncoordinated mess.

Dinah watched me with the detachment of a child watching a worm work its way across a sidewalk after a storm. "It's too bad it had to come to this," she said, her tone almost sad.

I wanted to answer, wanted to tell her I'd do whatever she wanted, but my mouth wouldn't work. Darkness was creeping into the edges of my vision, and I stilled, pressing my head to the rug and closing my eyes.

The last thing I heard before I lost consciousness was Chonks's angry yowl.

When I woke, I was so groggy for a minute I didn't realize that I was now sitting up. I attempted to stand, which was when I realized that I'd been tied to one of the heavy leather chairs in front of the library fireplace.

I blinked, taking in the scene around me. Dinah paced the rug much like I'd done earlier, muttering to herself. Although I hadn't known the woman for long, she'd always presented herself as being smart, professional, and driven. Now I could see that was only a façade. The cracks were showing, and the Dinah facing me now was half-crazed, talking to herself forcefully while obsessively clutching a ring of keys in her right hand.

It didn't take long for her to realize that I was awake. She came forward, crouching to look me in the eyes. "We could have done this the easy way, but I appreciate a tough negotiator," she said, her smile friendly as if she'd forgotten she'd drugged me and tied me to the chair.

I had no idea what she was talking about. "You should let me go," I said when my voice returned, albeit scratchy like a wool turtleneck. "You're not going to make this situation any better by hurting me."

Dinah laughed. "I think you're confused about the reality of this situation," she said. "You might think you drive a hard bargain, but I can assure you, I'm much harder."

"What is going on here?" I finally asked, unable to process her rambling. "What do you want? To shut me up? To keep me from going to the cops? Well, it's too late. Your cousin is already there, telling them everything."

Color drained out of Dinah's face. "What did you say?"

I bit my lip as I suddenly realized she wasn't here because she'd found out I was snooping around, trying to find out who really murdered Tabby Means. My best option was to play it off and bring the subject back to the real reason she was here.

"I... I don't know. I'm still groggy from whatever you shoved into my arm. What bargain are you talking about?"

Her face was shuttered, but she still replied. "For this house. You wouldn't let me buy it from you, so now I'll buy it from your estate."

My eyes widened. Had Dinah just threatened to kill me because I wouldn't sell her my house? "You're serious."

"As an open house with a full seafood buffet. We're going to close this deal tonight."

"You can have it," I said, fear making me quake. "I'll sign the house over to you. Just let me go."

Dinah chuckled. "So you can go back on your word the minute the ink dries? I think I'll just wait until after you're in the ground. I'll be able to pick up the house for a song, and I won't have to worry about you involving the authorities. Like my cousin has apparently."

It seemed my change of subject wasn't enough to make Dinah forget what I'd said about Patrick. She might be crazed, but she wasn't stupid. Putting the pieces together wouldn't take long, and I knew my chances of living through this were slim.

"Why do this?" I asked, figuring there was no reason not to ask. This was my chance to get the story straight from the perpetrator's own lips. "Why murder people just to get their properties? I know it's not a vast scheme to make a killing in the real estate market."

Dinah scoffed. "I've told you my plan, but you clearly had no faith in me, like all the others. I'm going to build the best historical museum anyone has ever seen, and it's going to bring tourists from all around to our little town, to see the past come to life."

"Yes, your historical museum. But you can't do that without Vince's cooperation, right?"

Scowling, Dinah straightened, putting her hands on her hips. "You're smarter than I gave you credit for. That, or you're nosier."

"Vince said he wasn't going to sell to you, so it seems like your museum dream was going to stay just that. A dream." I knew it was risky, talking to her like this, but I didn't care anymore. I was going to learn the truth about Tabby's death, even if it was the last thing I did.

And it looked like it just might be.

"That's where you're wrong," she said. "Vince is going to sell to me. I've already ensured that I'll get the property I need."

Remembering the map, I asked her how she figured he'd leave his family's land and the house generations of Means had occupied just for her dream. Dinah shook her head. "Maybe you aren't so smart. I don't want the Means estate. It's a lovely house, but it's just another plantation house. My ambition is bigger."

My brow furrowed, considering what she'd said. Picturing the county map from the records office, I went over in my mind the properties belonging to the Mercers. I'd assumed she planned to build the museum on the area of overlap between the Means land and the plot belonging to the Mercers. If Dinah wasn't interested in the Means property, however, then she must be planning to build somewhere else.

Patrick said she was trying to get the property at the end of the block. And the only other place where the Mercers and the Means owned property side by side was...

The realization hit me, and I couldn't believe I hadn't seen it earlier. "You're going to build downtown. You don't want the Means' estate. You want American Auto Garage."

Dinah crossed her arms over her chest, considering me like an animal trainer might consider a clever seal learning to clap her fins together for fish. "That's right. I'm going to rebuild New Orleans, the way it was when my family founded this town. But instead of another plantation house like the myriad folks can see all up and down the river, I'm going to have a whole block of historical buildings. They'll be staffed by docents in costume, and folks can shop, eat, and breathe history. It will be a gold mine."

"You're forgetting one little thing," I said. "Vince Means vowed to never sell to you."

"I haven't forgotten anything. Why do you think I killed Tabby Means? Vince is going to sell, and in fact, he'll thank me for taking the property off his hands."

CHAPTER 27

Dinah moved toward the long table behind the sofa, where I could see her purse was sitting. She dropped the ring of keys inside, then fished around in the purse's contents. I heard the unmistakable rattle of pill bottles. I knew then that there wasn't much time left, but I still hadn't figured out all of Dinah's plan.

She was obsessed with history, obsessed with bringing New Orleans back to the way it had been. Dinah didn't see her wicked scheme as stealing from others but as reclaiming what had once belonged to her family. She was righting a wrong, turning back the clock, reversing the Mercer's decline.

But why Tabby? She'd already had a tarnished reputation around town. How did killing Tabby help restore the Mercer name?

"If you wanted to make Vince sell to you, why murder Tabby? Why not kill Vince and buy the property you wanted from his estate?"

She frowned as she continued to dig in her purse. "Because if Vince dies, the Means properties get tied up in a trust that is divided between the remaining Means family. The rot runs deep in that family. I knew they'd be fighting over their shares for ages, locking the properties up in probate. By the time they hit the market, it would be too late."

"But what role did Tabby's death play? I still don't understand why you'd waste time killing her."

Dinah scoffed. "She was a distraction. Vince might have seen reason if he wasn't so concerned with that little hellion. But that wasn't the only reason taking her out was convenient."

She came forward, a bottle of pills in her hand. I knew that my continued existence depended on stalling her for as long as I could. I tried to follow her logic. Why would she benefit from having Tabby out of the way?

"If you were trying to force Vince's hand, why not leave Tabby's body at home where he might be blamed for the crime? With Vince in prison, it might be easier to convince him to sell to you."

Shaking her head, she continued her approach. "Vince would never go down for killing Tabby unless the sheriff himself saw him pull it off, and even then, it was iffy. Vince has the deepest pockets in town, meaning he can afford expensive lawyers to fight back for him. Those lawyers would be sure to work hard on figuring out who the real murderer was, which meant I would be more likely to get caught."

"Then why dump Tabby's body and stage a suicide that you knew everyone would see through?"

Dinah laughed. "I wanted them to see through it. I wanted them to think someone had killed her, probably Vince. You see, I didn't need him to go down for the crime, just to have enough people believe that he could have done it. The scandal would do my work for me."

I thought about what she was saying and realized suddenly how it could work. "You chose the auto garage to dump the body so that people would associate it with the murder."

"Correct. A thing like that works well to drive down property values. And if everyone in town started calling it 'the place where Vince dumped his wife's body,' it might suddenly sound like a good idea to Vince to sell it to me and let me tear it all down."

Eyes wide, all I could do was shake my head. The depth of her plan was awe inspiring. "How did you do it? How did you get close enough to Tabby without her realizing what you were planning?"

"Easy. The same way I got close to you. I just let myself in the back door."

"You have a key to my house," I said lamely. "Of course. Your cousin built it, right?"

Nodding, Dinah's smile was sweet. "That's right. You'd be surprised how much of this town used to belong to my family." I didn't have the heart to tell her I wouldn't be. After all, I'd seen the records myself. "So don't feel bad. I have keys to lots of places. Including the Means mansion."

"But the Means place never belonged to the Mercers," I pointed out.

"Correct. The key came from my Great Aunt Olivia Mercer, who became Great Aunt Olivia Means a few generations ago. Her children donated a few boxes of her things to the historical preservation society, and among her possessions were a couple keys. Very fortuitous keys. I added them to my collection. You'd be surprised how many people have random keys laying around. I've been collecting them since I was a child."

And now her collection was large and diverse enough that she was able to enter a variety of buildings around New Orleans. Homes. Businesses. It was a disturbing thought. I thought about Dinah as a girl and the determination she must have had, trying all keys she'd collected, figuring out which key matched which lock. A lifetime of letting herself into places she didn't belong.

"You left the book club meeting and headed for the Means mansion."

"I did." A cloud passed over her face. "The girl was unstable, and she'd just displayed it in front of a roomful of people at the book club meeting. I figured it was as good a time as ever to carry out the plan. But I hadn't expected the boy from the grocery store to be there."

Stanley "Taz" Lane, in the wrong place at the wrong time, I thought. What I said was, "Tabby lured him over with a promise of a ride home."

Dinah nodded. "I parked at the cabin, the one on my land, and walked over to the Means place, letting myself in the back door and making my way to where Tabby was, but I was surprised to see him there. She was draping herself all over him, and I could hear the liquor in her voice. So when she chased him around the house, I took the opportunity to pour some liquid lights-out in her drink."

Dinah stared out the window, her eyes far away as if she were replaying that night in her mind. "The boy wouldn't do what she wanted, something along the lines of being caught in bed with another man. He was so scared, he ran out of the house shirtless." Her mirthful smile made my stomach knot.

"After she was stumbling around from the tranquilizer, it was easy enough to herd Tabby into her car. It was late by then, so there were no cars on the road. I drove her to the garage, used a key from a set I'd already stolen from the Means house and copied months ago to unlock the building, then drove her inside."

Her tone was neutral while she looked straight into my eyes. "She was already cold by the time I tugged her over into the driver seat. There were enough odds and ends in the shop to stage her death as a suicide. All I had to do was start her car and make sure the garage was locked up tight."

Her dispassionate voice gave me chills. I thought I'd feel a sense of satisfaction once the mystery was solved, but it was missing. All I felt was disgust and sadness. Still, all the pieces were in place, save one.

Dinah opened the bottle, emblazoned with the name "Mercer Drug," and started shaking some pills into her hand. "You're going to swallow these, and then you're going to go to sleep. No fuss, no muss."

"Just one more thing. Taz's shirt. Why leave it in the car? Now the sheriff is pinning the murder on Taz, which means your scandal won't do its job."

"It will. I've already heard whispers around town, doubting that poor Stanley could do something like this. In fact, you and your friends are being very vocal about your doubts, raising awareness all around town to the fact that things don't add up."

I couldn't believe it. I had played right into Dinah's hand by working to free Taz. All the time I thought I was helping to bring

Tabby's killer to light, I was instead aiding Dinah in her nefarious plans.

"Open up," she said, moving the handful of pills toward my mouth. "You'll fall asleep, and soon enough, someone will find your body. They'll figure you were depressed, lonely in a new town and still grieving over the death of your uncle. No one might believe that Tabby Means would commit suicide, but I don't think we'll have that problem with you."

I started to struggle inside, attempting to break free from the chair she'd bound me to. "You can have my house," I said. "I'll give you the deed and leave town. You can add it to your tour or sell it to help fund your museum project. Just let me go, and it's yours."

"You're smarter than that," Dinah said. "And you know I am too. So stop making false promises and take your medicine."

I closed my mouth up tight and moved my face from side to side, but Dinah wrapped her arm around my head and used her hand to pinch my nose shut, cutting off my air. "You're going to have to open up. Why make this any harder on yourself than it has to be?"

I held my breath for as long as I could, but eventually, I had to open my mouth to get some air. I opened it as little as possible, but Dinah was able to get a finger between my lips. Tossing the pills into my mouth, she crowed in victory—until I spit the pills back into her face.

"Listen, you," she said, her tone stern. "You're going to swallow these damn pills. If you keep fighting me, I'm going to knock you out first, then feed the pills to you myself. You won't wake up again. I'm trying to give you some dignity, but I won't hesitate."

I spit another pill at her, energized when it hit her in the chest. I struggled harder against the ties that bound me. "I'm not going to cooperate in my own murder, thank you very much."

"Fine," she said, putting the cap back on the pill bottle. "We'll do it the hard way. I want to make sure these pills dissolve so there's no doubt of suicide, but I can knock you out and then shove them down your throat if that's what you want."

She pulled a hypodermic out of her purse and a large bottle half-full of clear liquid. I watched as she stuck the needle into the bottle's end and started filling it. I fought like hell to get out of that chair, but I couldn't avoid the needle when she pushed it into my bicep. It was in that moment that I knew for certain I was going to die.

It was also at that moment that my beloved Sir Chonksworth the Bold came to my rescue.

A flash of black and white fur rushed into the room, heading straight for my attacker. Chonks dug his claws in deep, right on Dinah's leg, and she let out a screech of pain. As she tried to remove my four-legged hero, I summoned all the strength I had left to yell for help at the top of my lungs.

The drug was taking effect, quicker than even last time, and I knew that soon I'd be under. These were likely the last few moments of my life, and they were full of desperation and fear.

Then I heard a crash, like splintering wood, and the heavy thump of footsteps heading in our direction. Through blurry eyes that were quickly closing, I saw a figure rushing into the library.

And then I saw nothing.

CHAPTER 28

"Good morning, Sleeping Beauty."

I blinked my eyes open, squinting into the light. I discovered that I was resting in my own bed, with Char sitting next to me. She had a stethoscope to her ears and was holding it to my wrist while she checked my blood pressure with a cuff.

"What happened?" I asked, feeling like my head was stuffed with cotton.

"What happened is you solved your first murder mystery, my dear." Her voice was too cheerful for whatever time of day it was.

I groaned. "My first? It better be my only. I don't think I could take another one." It was rushing back to me, what had happened with Dinah in the library. "Did someone—did they arrest her?"

Char nodded. "She's gone. Taken down to the station. And you'll be pleased to know that Stanley has already been released."

I smiled and let out a breath of relief. I might have been an inch away from death's door, but it hadn't been for nothing.

A sudden visitor landed on the end of my bed. Chonks rushed toward me, bumping his face into my cheek and letting out a meow of greeting. I held him close as he rubbed his face against mine, letting me know that he loved me more than he let on.

"There's my hero," I crooned. "Someone is going to get their favorite treat tonight. How's a big spoonful of yogurt sound?"

Chonks started to purr, collapsing onto my chest and rolling onto his side for belly scratches. Char pressed a tissue to her nose, chuckling at Chonks's antics.

"You better save some yogurt for Ethan. He's the one who broke down your front door and stopped Dinah from… well, you know."

My eyes widened. "Ethan?"

"Yeah. He's in the hall with my brother." Char jerked her thumb over her shoulder at the doorway, where I could see the handyman in conversation with Sheriff Rains.

"Can you believe that it was Dinah this whole time?" Char said, shaking her head. "Talk about unexpected."

"She was serious about that museum," I replied. "Serious enough to kill for it."

"But why Tabby Means? She didn't give a fig about history."

I told her how Dinah had planned to manipulate Vince into offloading the auto garage by means of a scandal. It was impressive how effectively she'd framed Vince for murder without actually framing him.

"That all makes sense. Except for Taz. Why was his T-shirt in the car if Dinah wanted suspicion to eventually fall on Vince?"

That bit had been bugging me too. "Taz said that Tabby took his shirt and shoved it down her skirt to keep him from getting it back, right?"

Char nodded. "Pretty effective trick."

"And Taz left shirtless that night. I've heard it from several people now, including Taz himself."

"Right."

Then it hit me. "What if Dinah didn't know where the shirt was? What if it was still stuffed inside of Tabby's skirt, and Dinah didn't notice it?"

I continued, remembering what Dinah had revealed. "Dinah said she helped Tabby into the car. Then at the garage, she'd moved her body over to the driver seat. Maybe the shirt had fallen out then, without Dinah noticing it. That's how it could have been found by the sheriff later."

"A single piece of randomness in a carefully executed plan," Char said, "and look at all the havoc it wreaked."

"Look at it this way," I said. "If Taz's shirt hadn't shown up in the car, everything might have happened exactly as Dinah said. Vince would have taken a lot of heat. Even with Taz's arrest, he was still a suspect, not only to us but to others around town who spend their time speculating about town gossip."

"So are you saying that, in some strange way, it's a good thing that Tabby was a woman of loose morals?"

I bit back a laugh. "In this case, maybe it was."

Char stood, turning to the side to blow her nose. "I'm going to give you and Chonks some space for this love fest. Let me know if you experience any headaches or excessive drowsiness."

She left the room, putting her arm on her brother's arm as she went into the hall. "Come on, Sheriff. Let's finish this up at the station. Jade needs her rest. She can come make a statement tomorrow."

Rains nodded and moved off with his sister, presumably to make a departure. Ethan, however, moved forward and poked his head into my bedroom.

"How are you feeling?"

I gave him a smile. "Better. And I hear I have you to thank for it."

His grin had a tinge of sheepishness. "I'm sorry about your door. But don't worry. I've already patched it up and put it back on. I'll bring a new door over tomorrow for a more permanent repair."

"A door is a small price to pay for my rescue. Thank you for saving me. I appreciate it."

Ethan broke eye contact, and I thought for a moment there might be a slight blush on his cheeks. He quickly refocused the conversation. "You should really be thanking my assistant there. He's the real hero."

"He did attack Dinah for me," I said, scratching behind Chonks's ears.

"Not just that, but I think he came to get me to, uh, to come rescue you." Ethan looked even more embarrassed than before.

"What do you mean?"

Ethan walked around the side of my bed and started vigorously scratching Chonks's head, making Chonks preen in happiness. "This big man here suddenly showed up at my place. I was out back, sanding some boards, when he comes running up, yowling his head off. I figured he wasn't supposed to be so far from home, so I put him in the car to bring him back over here to you."

Chonks stood up to get better leverage against the pets, then threw himself down again, this time on my stomach, knocking some of the air out of me.

"When we got to your place, he shot out of the car before I could catch him and ran off. I figured I better let you know what was going on, which is how I was on your front porch when I heard you scream for help. I broke the door down, and, well, here we are."

"Except one of us wouldn't be here if you hadn't shown up when you did." I looked down at Chonks. "How did you manage it, you big dummy? I thought the only thing that interested you was food."

"He's got to have some kind of secret exit somewhere in this old house that lets him come and go as he pleases. Otherwise, he couldn't have gotten out to run to my house or gotten back in to attack Dinah."

I nodded. "He's a lard butt, but his brain is almost as big as his belly." I didn't mention that his heart was twice the size of both put together.

"I still can't believe that Dinah Mercer was behind this whole thing. The sheriff said she planned to make it look like you were committing suicide, all so she could buy your house. I know real estate is supposed to be crazy, but I didn't take it so literally."

I laughed, then told him all about Dinah's plans for New Orleans and her own family's glory. Ethan whistled at the end of it, expressing his appreciation for the complication and precision inherent in her scheme.

"Now, I know this is going to sound bad, but I'm kind of disappointed that Dinah didn't manage to pull off the museum."

I looked at him, eyes wide in surprise, and he chuckled, saying he knew how it sounded. "But I would have made a killing as the lead contractor on the job. It's my skillset exactly, and I could have charged her extra for keeping quiet about any skeletons I uncover."

I shook my head. "What's to say she wouldn't just off you once she was finished, to save a few bucks?"

Ethan laughed. "I'd just make sure my buddy Chonks was around to protect me." Chonks let out a small mewl as if he understood everything Ethan was saying and agreed.

"It's still amazing that someone like Dinah would be able to do something as disturbing as all this." His earlier levity gone, Ethan struggled to express what he was feeling. "She was a colleague, someone I'd worked with many times through the historical preservation society and because she'd used me and recommended me for other projects. I interacted with this woman several times a week for years, and I never would have thought her capable of what she's done."

"I had no hint of it either," I said, putting my hand on his in a gesture of comfort. "We talked several times, even here in my own house. I never for one moment thought she'd be tying me up and trying to force me to overdose on sleeping pills."

Ethan took my hand and squeezed it. "It must have been very frightening."

"It was," I said, squeezing it back. "But I'm all right now."

"I suppose everyone has a side they keep to themselves."

"I suppose you're right." I told Ethan about the ring of keys and Dinah's collection and how she could creep around almost anyone's house anytime she liked.

"That's unsettling. Not to mention unethical."

"And illegal," I reminded him.

He'd just opened his mouth to reply when the sound came. It reverberated through the walls, the screaming sound of metal against metal combined with the rhythmic tapping.

"The ghost?" he asked when the sound had subsided.

I nodded. "I wasn't making it up."

He laughed. "I never thought you were."

Blushing, I shrugged.

Ethan looked at me, a tiny smile on his face, and his gaze filled me with warmth. "Let me go see if I can locate your ghost for you, since I'm here."

I reclined against my pillows, petting Chonks and coming to grips with my near-death experience. I'd expected a more sedate life in the Old South. Long, sultry days and quiet country nights.

What I hadn't expected was to face a cold-blooded killer in my own home. One who had murdered once and wasn't afraid to do it again. That was something that seemed more likely on the streets of Baltimore than in the backwoods of Louisiana. Maybe I was too narrowminded in my thinking.

Should I pack it all up now, go back to the relative safety of my old home?

"No," I said aloud to Chonks. "This is our home now, and no murderer or ghost is going to scare us off."

"Not a ghost," Ethan said from the hallway. He re-entered the bedroom, his hands cupped. "Somehow, this guy had gotten into an old dumbwaiter system." Approaching the bed, he cracked open his hands a sliver so I could see inside.

It was a little gray mouse, its nose twitching, its furry little body trembling. Chonks stood up for a sniff, and Ethan pulled his hands back.

"How did that little thing make all those big sounds?"

"It's interesting. There used to be a dumbwaiter that ran from the basement, past the kitchen, and into the hall outside this room. Someone walled it in years ago, but this little guy managed to trap himself in there. He could scrabble up and down between the floors on the rope, but sometimes, he managed to actually move the dumbwaiter box, which caused the screeching sound in the pulley gears, and the rhythmic tapping was from the unbalanced box hitting against the wall."

"It's a good thing you found him," I said. "He could have starved back there."

"I doubt that," Ethan replied. "Our ghost here is actually rather plump. My guess is he was feeding off the scraps of Chonks's food that rolled into the small crevice near the kitchen floor. That's likely how he got back there too, through that same crack. I can fix it up for you, or better yet, repair the dumbwaiter so it functions again."

I looked at Chonks, who was staring back at me. "What do you say, Chonks? Should we have Ethan come back over and do some more work for us?"

Chonks flopped over, exposing his belly for rubbing and purring like crazy. Ethan and I both laughed. "I guess that's my answer."

EPILOGUE

It was another painfully humid day, and my fur frizzed all around me, making me resemble a wad of cotton photographed in black and white.

I was lying on the porch, hanging out with my roommate and her friend. Things had died down since the craziness of last week, in which I had to save the town from a murderer, but it was still all anyone could talk about.

Me? It bored me. How many times could you hear about your own valor before it became stale?

"I still don't know why Dinah would do it," Char was saying from one of the two rocking chairs. "I've been thinking about it all week, what it would take for me to actually murder another human being. How Dinah could have gotten to that place, I may never understand."

Jade nodded from her rocking chair. "It would have to be some need inside her that was stronger than her fear. And fulfilling that need would have to have been worth the risk many times over."

"But a museum?" Char asked, grimacing. "I mean, I'm a doctor, so I think you can say I'm fairly deep in nerd territory—"

Jade nodded, murmuring, "The librarian agrees."

Char laughed at the interruption. "But even for a nerd like me, a museum isn't something I could see killing for. I mean, Dinah was on the level of Indiana Jones here, but even he wasn't a cold-blooded killer."

"Except maybe if you count Nazis," Jade countered.

"Well, okay, maybe not Nazis, but still—"

"I know what you mean." Jade considered the question. "But maybe it wasn't the museum or just the museum. Maybe it was more of what it represented. A legacy." She sat forward, getting into her argument. "I mean, think about it. Dinah isn't married. She doesn't have any children. And if the records I dug through at City Hall are right, she's one of the few left in the area that still carries the Mercer name."

Char rocked slowly in thought. "Patrick is also a bachelor with no kids. I guess as one of the last of her line, she might have seen herself as the final line of defense. If she did nothing, her family's name would fade into history. But a museum complex that bore her family's name would ensure the Mercers were remembered."

"That might be enough to give her life meaning," Jade said.

"And enough to end the lives of others," Char said, a shiver going through her.

I stood, leaping into Char's lap to let her know I agreed and to see if I could get a sneeze out of her. Humans and their weaknesses were so amusing.

"Oh, Chonks," she said, letting out a grunt as I forced the air out of her lungs. "You're a healthy boy, aren't you?"

I swished my tail under her nose, eliciting the sneeze I was waiting for. I was quick to jump out of the way before it could hit me as collateral damage.

"Chonks, you have to stop doing that or Char won't come to visit anymore."

"Yeah," Char piled on. "Meaning I won't sneak you little bits of pepperoni when I bring a pizza with me."

"You do that?" Jade asked, indignant.

I sat on my haunches to see where this would go.

"Just a little," Char said, scrunching her shoulders in glee. "I want to make sure he likes me."

"For god sakes, woman, you're a medical doctor! You know what pepperoni could do to a cat. Lord knows he's fat enough."

"Cats can have a little pepperoni," Char said with a smile and a shrug.

Jade rolled her eyes, leaning back and groaning to the ceiling. "You two will be the death of me."

"I can just see your tombstone now. 'She died as she lived. Annoyed.'"

Jade laughed, and it was a good sound. Although I'd had my doubts initially about moving to this muggy municipality, this little Louisiana town had grown on me. It seemed that my roommate felt much the same.

"New Orleans isn't like I expected," she mused.

"I told you, people down south are just as messed up as folks in the rest of the country. We have our secrets and our lies. Just look at the screwed-up relationship between Tabby and Vince. There were two people who were lying to themselves as much as they were lying to each other."

Jade sighed. "I find myself feeling sorry for Tabby. She came to the book club hoping to impress her husband, to make herself fit into his mold for his perfect wife. But Tabby realized it was an impossible task, so she reverted back to her bad behaviors, encouraging petty jealousy and in-fighting."

"Don't feel too sorry for her," Char said. "I don't like to speak ill of the dead, but Tabby left a ton of misery in her wake. Look at what she did to Taz. She threatened to evict her own mother. And she had no problems stealing Mercy's husband."

"Mercy's husband didn't seem to mind being stolen," Jade countered.

Char accepted the point. "Vince isn't blameless either. I completely agree." She paused. "It's like in *Gatsby*. Tom and Daisy, the careless people who used everyone else as toys to be played with against their backdrop of boredom or entitlement."

I thought of the line she was referring to and thought Fitzgerald put it better when he said, "they smashed up things and creatures and then retreated back into their money or their vast carelessness or whatever it was that kept them together, and let other people clean up the mess they had made."

Other people like Jade and Char, like Taz who'd just chosen the wrong time to try and open up to others. People like Mercy and Gita and Tammy, imperfect women who nevertheless didn't deserve the pain they were brought.

"The most important thing is that Taz is free," Char reminded her friend. "And from what I heard today, Vince is getting a taste of his own medicine."

"Do share," Jade said, and I perked up my ears for this latest piece of town gossip.

"Vince was suing Mercy over her alimony, claiming that she was having an affair while they were still married. His proof? Tammy Carter's testimony that she'd seen Jimmy and Mercy carrying on before the divorce."

"Ah ha!" Jade said, raising an index finger to the ceiling. "So that's why Vince didn't want to evict her. And it must be the real deal that Tammy was talking about. The one she said was for her food truck but that we both knew was malarkey."

Char nodded. "It gets better. When it came time for Tammy to testify, she couldn't. She said she didn't care if she ended up homeless, but she was tired of all the deceit. Mercy didn't start seeing Jimmy until after the divorce, and furthermore, Vince tried to pay her by knocking off some of the back rent she owed to lie for him."

My roommate started to clap as Char continued. "The judge dismissed the case, and even said he'd be referring the case to the parish prosecutor to consider charges for Vince himself."

The girls continued their conversation, trading barbs about the kind of punishment they'd mete out for Vince if they were the judge, but I quickly lost interest. Stretching, I clambered down the porch steps and into the yard. Jade wasn't paying any attention, so I could enjoy the short breath of freedom she was offering. Besides, I could use some behind the ear scratches, and I knew where to find the best ones.

As I ambled around the corner of the house, I congratulated myself once again on solving the mystery of the dead trophy wife. It was almost painful, having to watch my roommate flounder around from clue to clue, making mistake after mistake. It was almost enough to make me throw up a hairball just watching her waste time and effort.

I couldn't blame the humans. Their sense of smell was just so pitiful when compared to my superior species. If Jade could smell like I could, she would have smelled the medicine in Dinah's purse during that first book club meeting. That same smell was present at the crime scene, which I just happened to stumble upon when making my rounds of the new town.

And it was the same smell I'd caught a whiff of when the homicidal woman had come out of the building with the glowing green sign and the giant eyes in the window. I'd seen her on my first jaunt around New Orleans, and I'd wondered what she was doing, creeping around a closed storefront in the middle of the night.

I had done my best to give Jade all the signals she needed to solve the crime. But humans were just so darn slow sometimes. How much more of a clue did she need than me burying Dinah's card in my litter box? That is the ultimate insult among cat-kind.

Catching sight of Ethan's plaid shirt, I hustled up to where he was crouched next to the side of the house.

"Hey, buddy," he said, scratching me in the way only he could.

I rubbed all over him as best I could, marking him as mine.

Ethan rubbed my back. "I think I found your escape hatch," he said, pointing to the broken basement window I'd been using as a cat door for the past couple months. "I'm pretty sure Jade is going to ask me to repair this. Then you'll be out of luck, bud."

I bristled, angry at being denied my sovereign right to freedom. Still, I knew that if he blocked this exit, I'd just find another one. The old plantation house was a wonderland of warrens and hidden passages, after all.

Running after him, I climbed on the porch just as he announced his finding to my roommate.

"Oh yeah, we're going to have to fix that," Jade said, and I threw myself down at her feet, biting her toes in her sandals.

"Chonks, you're a crazy person!" she yelped, pulling her toe out of my grasp. "I wonder how many adventures you've been on since you found that broken window."

I looked up at her, my expression as innocent as could be. She'd find out soon enough about my latest adventure. I had already ferreted out another secret, one that has been buried for almost a decade. But it wouldn't be long before that secret was brought to light.

I wondered how the town would take it, when one lie after another would be exposed. And even those who seemed innocent were found to have blood on their hands.

Would Jade still fight for her friends if she knew about the skeletons in their closets… or their backyards?

Ethan stooped to run his hand down my back and I forgot all about the dark thoughts swirling around in my head. This was a man who was excellent with his hands. There had to be a way to get him to come over more often. I'd thought the trick with the mouse would work for months, but clever human that he was, he'd figured it out.

Maybe it was time to break something else…

THE END

ABOUT THE AUTHOR

B.K. is a pen name for a couple of good friends who love reading a good mystery and are as cheeky as they come. Murder She Wrote was one of their favorite childhood shows and there wasn't a day that went by that they were getting into trouble looking for a mystery in the neighborhood to solve. With a ton of ideas and imagination, you're in for a funny wild ride.

They live in Texas and enjoy BBQ and sweet tea more than anyone should become aware of!

Come connect and join the fun!

Printed in Great Britain
by Amazon

68874487R00123